# MINE

A STREET WHERE YOU LIVE SUSPENSE

ANDREA M. LONG

This book is a work of fiction. Names, characters, places and incidents are either the product of the author's imagination or are used fictitiously, and any resemblance to actual persons, living or dead, events or locales is entirely coincidental.

No part of this book may be reproduced or transmitted in any form or by any means, electronic or mechanical, including photocopying, recording or by any information storage and retrieval system without the written permission of the author, except for the use of brief quotations in a book review.

The author, Andrea M. Long, does not consent to any Artificial Intelligence (AI), generative AI, large language model, machine learning, chatbot, or other automated analysis, generative process, or replication programme to reproduce, mimic, remix, summarise, or otherwise replicate any part of this creative work, via any means.

The author supports the right of humans to control their artistic works. No part of this book has been created using AI-generated images or narrative, as known by the author.

Copyright (c) 2017 by Andrea M. Long

All rights reserved.

Cover photo from Adobe Stock. Cover design by T. Clarke.

## AUTHOR'S NOTE

This book is written in British English and is set in the U.K.

My psychological suspense reads contain flawed characters and situations that are all the more disturbing for the fact they could happen in real life.

# PART 1

## MELISSA

# CHAPTER ONE

## SAM

30 August 2014

People are abhorrent. Before, I was tolerant, friendly, with the human emotion of wishing to be liked, adored even. I thought I was. What a stupid, ignorant bitch. Now as people talk, I watch their mouths twist into different shapes as they deliver their subjective wisdom. If only they knew that while I pick up on small phrases I can acknowledge with a small smile or a nod of my head, my mind visualises wrapping my hands around their neck and squeezing until their eyes bulge, blood vessels bursting, and they beg for their life.

Why not think of that the next time you speak to your friends. Is what you're saying so important that you'd fight to speak it if denied your breath?

I spend hours studying people. Like the fat woman who just stuffed half a pasty in her mouth with one great push of her hand. Don't judge me. I have no problem with anyone's appearance. I wasn't always this slim. What makes my face grimace is the inelegance of how she ate it. I want to force my fingers down her throat and make her throw up every morsel. I'd show her the regurgitated lumps where the food remained solid because she couldn't take the time to chew or taste her food. Then I'd make her eat it again, this time with style.

Then there are the clone-like faces of the technological revolution. Robotic on their bus seats. Tap, tap, tap, go their fingers. I'll sit near them, smirking. They're unaware of me considering how I could stab them, and they'd never see it coming. Their puckered mouths would form an 'O' as I smiled and rang the bell. I'd depart the bus, leaving them bleeding with no one the wiser as they're all too busy telling relatives they are on the bus, playing Candy Crush, or seeing what amazing statuses their fake friends have posted on social media. People they've never met get more acknowledgement than I do, although I travel with them every day.

But I distract myself. I have a story to tell. Because I wasn't always like this. Once, I was kind. Before *him*.


'S-Sam?'

I blink and come to. Remember where I am. I'd lost myself for a minute there.

I sigh. What sort of therapist stutters? Mine has sweat pouring down his face for fuck's sake.

The room is an ambient temperature. Light would enter the room from the small window if the blind wasn't closed. My fingers grip the edge of my chair as I attempt to control myself.

My therapist wipes the sweat off his forehead with a shaky hand. He disgusts me. He needs a good wash.

'So, Sam. Would you like to tell me why you are h-here?'

I smile. I should try to keep hold of my emotions, but I can't help myself. A laugh threatens to break. Instead, a smile hurts my cheek as it stretches my face.

'I think therapy will be so much fun. I can't wait to explore my fucked-up mind with you.'

A flash of terror crosses his face. A brief moment

before his cold mask returns. But that one glimpse of fear makes my pussy wet.

His Adam's apple rises and falls. 'So, you made this appointment Sam. Where do you want to begin?'

I push my tongue into my cheek and consider my position while I stare at him. Then I sit up straight, and a smirk teases the edge of my lips a second time. 'I'll tell you how I met Edward. I think that's as good a place as any to start.'

The adrenaline pumps through my veins. It feels good. It's been a long time since I felt in charge. Like I was winning.

# CHAPTER TWO

## SAM
July 2013

It's my first day of employment at Bailey's Accountants. The interview had been a breeze. Take a middle-aged man called Jacobs and present him with a slim, blue-eyed blonde. I'd run my fingers through my cropped hair. Thought about the questions asked while placing a finger against my perfect pout. I repeatedly flicked my tongue against perfect white teeth. Let's face it, he wasn't appraising me for the post, he imagined my mouth around his cock. I'd kept my skirt knee-length, but it still seemed inappropriate given the length of my legs. During the interview, I'd crossed and uncrossed my gym bunny calves so he could imagine them wrapped around him, squeezing out his orgasm. A perfectly orchestrated interview. I conducted myself impeccably, and so here I am – PA to Mr Edward Bonham. *Bon Homme*, good man. We'll see about that. I was surprised the man himself hadn't interviewed me but as I came to find out, assistants weren't that important to him.

I'm inducted to the job and given passwords to the computer systems. Introductions to other staff members are made. I've yet to work out who can assist me and who'll try to thwart me. Has he already fucked any of the staff here? Or does he keep his private life separate? That's what I'm here to discover.

First day. First mistake. I'm bawled out of his office for disturbing him before eight am. I'd thought I'd get brownie points for being early and efficient.

I storm into the staff room to get myself a drink of iced water. My hand shakes as I press and hold the ice button. Kerry, one of the other personal assistants, mistakes it for nerves rather than the murderous anger coursing through my veins.

'Did no one tell you about Mr Bonham's morning routine?' She bites on her bottom lip.

I smile widely at her. If she sees it doesn't reach my eyes, she doesn't let on. 'No, they didn't.'

'Gosh, sorry about that. Mr Bonham meditates for thirty minutes every morning. He's never to be disturbed. I think it's kind of like a ritual for him. Maybe he thinks it brings him luck? But for thirty minutes exactly, from eight to eight-thirty am he does it. Not one second outside of either time.'

I raise an eyebrow. 'So, I'm working for a weirdo?'

She shakes her head. 'No. You're working for one of the most focused men I've ever come across.'

I see the change in her pupils as she speaks of him. Girl crush o' clock.

I lean against the sink, blocking Kerry from filling the kettle in her hand. 'So, what's he really like? What do you think of him? Anything else I should be aware of?'

She stands and looks up at me through a thick fringe. 'There are some rumours about him. They're probably made up.'

I move away from the sink, giving her access to fill her kettle. 'Ooh, I love gossip. Tell me more.'

She bites her lip again as she turns the tap. Spray shoots out and wets her blouse. She sighs. 'I'm told he's just as focused in the bedroom as he is at work.'

'I thought he was married? He wears a ring.'

'He is. She's lovely. I think they're madly in love still. Have been since the day they met apparently, but there are rumours about his extra-curricular activities. I've never seen anything but devotion to his wife though.'

She gives another sigh, this time a dreamy one. 'Anyway, I'd better get back. Jack – Mr Simpson – he'll be wondering where his cup of tea is. I hope you enjoy your first day, Sam.'

I smile again before speaking. 'Thanks for the heads up. It's appreciated. It's hard being the new girl.'

She nods and leaves the room.

I pick up my drink of iced water, squeezing the plastic cup until it breaks apart in my hand. Water runs down my sleeve and drips onto the floor. I place ice in my mouth and hold it there until it burns my tongue. Pain. Now feeling focused, I throw the cup in the bin and return to the office.

Edward is six-foot-two. He has short dark hair, longer at the top and shaved at the sides. Every morning before work he trains in the gym. He has muscles on muscles. For a man who's going to turn fifty this year, he's in prime condition. Information gleaned because I've now been stalking him for a long time. I know many, many things about Mr Edward Bonham.

But I need to break into his inner circle. Being a watcher is not an option anymore. It's time for action.

I stroll into his office, with my head held high.

'So, Sam, just so we can be clear -'

I put my hand up. Palm facing him, fingers outstretched. 'I've been briefed. My apologies. I wasn't aware. I won't set foot in the office until after eight-thirty am from now on.'

He nods. 'Thank you.'

'Just one thing though.' I fix him with a direct stare. 'I can take orders. I like order and I adore routine. But don't ever raise your voice to me again.'

He raises an eyebrow. 'But I'm the boss.'

I tilt my head, meeting his steely gaze. 'There are ways to be a boss and losing control and shouting at staff isn't one of them. I observed part of your meditation this morning. You seem like someone who prefers order and control in their life?'

The corner of his mouth twists.

'You can tell that by the fact I meditate in the morning?'

'No. I can tell by the fact it has to start at eight am and end at eight-thirty am precisely. I can walk through that door at eight-thirty-one every morning should it please you.'

He gasps and covers it quickly with a cough before he relaxes back in his seat. 'A morning coffee anytime from eight-thirty to nine am is fine, depending on the meetings or work I have scheduled. I need my PA to be adaptable to my timetable.'

'Noted. I'll make you a coffee right now.'

I head out of the room, but I don't go straight to the staff room. I hover at the periphery of the door and watch him.

He sits with his hand on his chin, absentmindedly stroking his jaw. Then he shakes his head and switches on his computer.

I'm aware my own plans may take time. But that's not a problem. There's never been a rush.

Back at my flat that evening, I prepared my usual salad. I also have a strict routine. Nothing but water passes my lips. From work, I'd visited the gym where my personal trainer put me through my paces for an hour. My evening ritual consisted of removing my blue contact lenses and then moisturising every part of my skin to keep it in pristine, soft, and supple condition. Next was to check my hair for root growth and apply dye if necessary. I did thirty minutes of yoga before bed and then prepared my work clothes for the next day, hanging them on the back of the bathroom door. Everything had to be perfectly so. All worked out and ordered. For every day was an act, a stage I'd prepared myself for. The performance had started.

## Present Day - 30 August 2014

'So why did you want to ruin this man?' His voice is calm again, controlled, no stutter.

I snigger. 'You're not a very experienced therapist, are you?'

He looks at the floor.

'Mr Therapist, we have to get to the crux of the matter slowly. You're supposed to guide me towards discovering the answers for myself. I'm not just going to come out and tell you why I've done the things I've done.' I leap up. 'Do you know what? I don't think this relationship is going to work out.'

'No,' he says firmly, through gritted teeth. 'As you say, I'm the therapist. Let me direct you, and we'll find the answers together.'

I sit back in my seat and smile. It would seem my

therapist has found his balls. I'll delight in watching them retreat so far up he's in agony.

'Please continue, Sam. What happened next with Edward?'

I smirk. 'What indeed?'

## CHAPTER THREE

### SAM

I knew it would be difficult to get to Ed. His discipline and regimented life meant that he didn't have room for anything outside of work and home. This is where meticulous planning and research came in. I had to know exactly what buttons to push to get him to consider something outside of his schedule, painstakingly plotted out in his electronic diary. Luckily, I have a friend, Bobby, who'll do anything for me.' My eyes drift towards the blind. 'He's a friend I made some time ago. We'll discuss him soon, but for now, all you need to know is that he's helped me a lot.'

Bobby made an appointment to see Ed. Under an assumed name of course. Ed was his usual highly professional self, taking his client out for dinner seeing as he looked like making a huge bonus from him. Then Bobby made a sexual harassment claim against Ed to Ed's boss, Jacobs.' I beam while I stare at my therapist. 'It was fantastic because meticulous, controlled Ed never fucks up and is so fucking loyal to his wife. His boss came to his office, and you could hear the raised voices all the way down the corridor. Aftershocks tore through the building's staff. Ed? Sexual harassment with another male? Surely there was some mistake. Wasn't he happily married? I owe Bobby so, so much. He gave me my way in. Ed tried to track him down but of course, he couldn't because the customer didn't exist. The damage was done anyway, because there's no smoke without fire, right? Staff chatted behind his back for weeks. He loathed it. I'd see him snap pencils while sitting at his desk, his jaw set and his mind deep in thought.'

I drift into past memories as I recount the story.

*After a few minutes, I went into the office unsure of what I would find.*

'Mr Bonham? I heard the commotion. Is there anything I can—?'

'You can get the fuck out of my office, that's what you can do,' he snarled.

I slammed my hand on his desk. 'I warned you I wouldn't be spoken to like that. I've not fucked up here.'

His eyes widened. 'My, Ms Briers, you certainly take risks, confronting an angry man. What if I'd have lost my temper completely?'

I shook my head. 'I don't think you would. I think you know how to regain that control and harness it for use in other ways.'

He turned away, swivelling his chair towards the window. 'You know nothing about me.'

I spoke to the back of his head, my voice low in tone. 'I've seen how you are in your workspace, but you're right. I don't know anything about you. But I'm good at reading people. You like control. Today you lost it, for that brief moment when Mr Jacobs came in here. Now you'll claw it back. I bet you already have a scheme in your head on how to get your client to retract their complaint. I know you want Jacobs in here on his knees, apologising.'

Edward turned his chair around and narrowed his gaze. 'You're an intriguing assistant, Ms Briers. That's a lot you assume about me. Perhaps you have a crush and *are building me up as a hero in your mind. It wouldn't be the first time it's happened. Women like a man in a position of power.'*

*I stood my ground. 'Don't belittle me or flatter yourself. Psychology interests me, yes. I did an A-level in the subject, and I watch programmes about it too. Watching your control is fascinating, but don't think for one minute I'd let you take me to bed. I'm not attracted to you so don't worry about any crushes here.'*

*His jaw tightened, then relaxed. 'Only my wife has been in my bed.'*

*'How lovely, and so rare these days. I hope she's as faithful as you are.'*

*He jumped back in his seat.*

*'What the hell-?'*

*My smirk returned. 'I'm just testing. I told you, I like studying people. Searching for their reactions.'*

*'You'd be as well not studying me.' A threat lay unspoken within his tone.*

*'Just make sure you treat me with the same respect you do all your other business associates, and we'll be fine. Now, I'll leave you to concentrate on what you're going to do to Jacobs.'*

*He opens a clenched fist and massages his fingers with his other hand. 'Why are you so interested in Jacobs?'*

*'Because something tells me it will be extraordinary. I get bored so easily, Mr Bonham. I've been unable to settle to any kind of career because I find most of my employment so mind-numbingly dull. Don't let me get bored here. I'm starting to enjoy myself.'*

'Call me Ed,' he says.

'For all his control, a simple bit of flattery at a weak moment and I had my way in.'

'What about guilt? Do you feel guilt over your actions?' my therapist asks.

'Everything I've done has been justified as far as I'm concerned. He didn't deserve to be happy, to have a happy marriage. I've taken from them what was taken from me. Why should they enjoy what I was denied?'

'How do you know they were happy? Most married couples have fucked-up lives behind closed doors.'

'Well, they thought they had it all. I witnessed enough of it.'

'Maybe you only saw what you wanted to see?'

I exhale deeply, my nostrils flaring.

'Perhaps we should move on. Maybe you could tell me something of your family? What were your parents like?'

At this, I laugh hysterically. Once I begin, I can't

stop. Tears trail down my face and my jaw hurts from laughing so hard. 'Is that what you think therapy is? The psychotic have fucked-up childhoods that explain everything?'

He blanches. I watch another drop of sweat trickle down his cheek. I walk over to him, lean in, and lick it off his face.

He does his best to hold still. To give me no satisfaction from my action. Kudos. I'd have punched me.

I sit on the edge of the desk, peering down at him.

'I had an amazing childhood. My parents weren't rich by any stretch of the imagination, but they provided for me the best they could. I was loved. I had amazing toys. Fabulous holidays at the beach. I visited them twice a week until they died.'

'You lost your parents? You must have been very young. You can only be in your twenties now?'

'How and when I lost my parents is not something I'm willing to discuss. I'll get to it in due course.'

He sighs. 'I'm not sure what you want to get out of this therapy. Every time I ask you a question, you defer it, or you laugh at me. Is this all a joke?'

I narrow my eyes and lean toward him. 'It's far from a joke. I just thought it would be good for us to chat. In a controlled environment.'

'For how long? How long is this therapy session

going to last? Can you answer me that question at least?'

He shakes his arm. The chain holding his right arm to the wall rattles. He's losing control. I don't know how much longer I can keep him here.

'It will take as long as it takes.'

He glares at me as his urine gushes down his leg and onto the floor. My punishment for his subordination.

I display no reaction. I leave the room, returning with a bucket, warm soapy water and a change of trousers. I don't speak to him again for the rest of the day.

## CHAPTER FOUR

MELISSA
February 1985

We move into our new home on the twentieth of February nineteen eighty-five. Number twenty-three Cyclamen Crescent. A beautiful name for a beautiful crescent of houses. As a self-employed electrician, Jarrod has built a reliable reputation, leaving many almost dependent on his services. This has meant I've stayed home to be a housewife. To cook, clean, care for him and to do the same for our children when they arrive.

Jarrod and I were childhood sweethearts. We met

at nursery school, and our first wedding took place when we were six – in the year of decimalisation – with the class teacher as registrar and classmates as bridesmaids and guests. I doubt any of those people would believe we repeated the wedding and got married for real when we were the tender age of eighteen. Our wedding disco was filled with the sounds of Duran Duran, Spandau Ballet, and Culture Club.

After living with Jarrod's parents since we married, our new home is a diamond in a bed of coal. Jarrod has called in favours from his friends in the trade, and our house is stunning. I'm nervous about meeting the new neighbours, used to keeping out of the way and trying to be seen and not heard. It's strange when people come to our door to say hello and welcome us to the crescent. We're told it's always been a place where neighbours are close. They'll look out for us. Jarrod says that means they are nosy bastards, but I think it's sweet.

During the first week, I decide I'll bake and take my offerings around some of the neighbours. I'm not the best cook, but my baking's not so bad. I make several batches of jam tarts and place them in Tupperware boxes. I hope they'll give the boxes back - they were a wedding gift.

The first house I visit is Sandra's. I'm informed that

Sandra and her husband Dave have lived here for the past seven years. She invites me in for a cup of tea. I enter, looking around to see if any of the other neighbours' curtains are twitching as they watch me go inside. It seems that kind of street.

'I'm so glad you called around, honey. You've picked a lovely place to come and live. Everyone here is just so friendly. Are you newlyweds?'

I smile and take a sip of my hot tea. 'We've been married two years officially, fourteen if you count our nursery school ceremony.' I take a worn Polaroid picture out of my bag and show her myself and Jarrod at our first ceremony. Then I take out a further photo showing us at the proper wedding.

'Oh, that's just adorable. You are both beyond cute.'

'Thank you.'

'Right, let's have a couple of those jam tarts of yours to go with this tea.' She hands me a side plate and then my own Tupperware box. 'So, where did you live before then?'

'Since the wedding, we lived with Jarrod's parents. We had two rooms upstairs, one as a bedroom and one as a sitting room.'

'Newlyweds? Sharing with the folks. That must have been difficult if you get what I mean.' She titters.

I blush.

'Oh, I'm sorry; I didn't mean to embarrass you. That's the problem with us all getting on so well around here. We're used to joking with each other.'

'I'm sure I'll get used to it.' I shrug. 'As you say, it's just different at the moment. I kind of feel like a nursery school child again. Playing houses.'

'Believe me, the novelty will wear off when you've done the washing for the umpteenth time, and then your husband gets home and gives you yet another set of dirty overalls, or in Dave's case, cricket attire. That's such a pain in the backside to clean.'

I can't imagine ever being bored of seeing Jarrod's face when he smiles at me or when I bring him his meal or fold away his washing. As for the sex, we didn't have it too often seeing as we were in his parents' house, but that should change now, once we get settled. With all the hours Jarrod works and the fact he gets home late sometimes, I'm not going to annoy him about it. I know he loves me. He tells me every day. In the next few years, we're going to start a family. Jarrod just wants to get a little more of a nest egg behind us as the new house has wiped out a lot of our savings.

'So, once you're settled in, a couple of times a week the guys have a card game. They take it in turns as to which house they play at. We ladies get together for an hour or two for a chat. Sometimes we'll have a clothes party. That's if you're interested? I don't want you to feel forced into anything.'

'Oh no, that'll be lovely.' I tell her. 'I'll get to know the other women on the street quicker. Jarrod often works late, but I'm sure he'll try to join in.'

'Well, just so you know you are welcome anytime. Mmmm, these jam tarts are delicious, Mel.'

Only my father and Jarrod call me Mel, so I bristle at this over-familiarity. Then I chastise myself. She's being friendly. It's only a name.

I exhale. 'Oh, I'm pleased they're okay. I don't cook or bake very often. I was a little nervous they'd be too dry.'

'No, they're just right. If you want a few cooking lessons, I can teach you. I do a mean meat and potato pie. Will fill that husband up a treat. He'll be in your debt for days.'

I laugh. I like Sandra. She can only be about five years older than me. Maybe I'll get the nerve up to ask her the next time I see her. She's very maternal. I hear a wail.

'Oh hell, Joanne's awake. Those afternoon naps seem to fly.'

'I didn't realise you had a child.'

'Two of them. Becky's at school. She's five and Joanne is eighteen months. I bet it'll be your turn soon.'

'I hope so.' I confide in her.

'Would you like to meet Joanne? She might be a little grumpy at first, but once she's had a nappy change and a bottle, she should be good for a cuddle.'

'I'd love to.'

This becomes a regular event. The odd cooking lesson, a lot of chatter with Sandra, and cuddles with the baby. I feel instantly at home with Sandra.

Now and again I'm still around when Dave comes home from work. He's a banker and looks so rigid and formal in his suit that the first time I see him, I shrink back.

Then he clasps my hand in his and brings me in for a hug.

'So, this is the famous Mel I've heard so much about lately. My wife never shuts up about you.'

She elbows him and then goes off to make him a drink.

'Seriously, Mel,' he lowers his voice, 'Whatever you're doing, please keep doing it. I was worried she was getting a little lonely stuck in with the baby. You've brought a change to her since you started visiting.'

'That's great because I love coming around here. I was wondering if I might be overstaying my welcome.'

'Not at all. Not at all,' he tells me. 'Now, the next thing you need to do is to get Jarrod to one of our game nights. He's proving elusive.'

'He's just been really busy. I'll tell him. I'm sure he'll come along soon.'

'I hope so. I want to meet the man who is fortunate to have such a fantastic wife.'

I giggle, unsure how to handle the compliment.

'You're embarrassing her, Dave. It's true though. You are a very sweet person. Your Jarrod is lucky to have you. Now you better go and get his tea fixed, or he'll be calling us a bad influence.'

I see the time. Oh, my goodness, he could be home very soon. For once I pray that he is running late on a job, so I'm not caught out.

I rush home and reheat a spare pie I made yesterday. Sandra has been showing me batch cooking. Today it works perfectly. Her habits are rubbing off on me, as I spend more time cooking things that can be reheated to allow me to spend more time at Sandra's. Hey, isn't that what Tupperware is for?

## CHAPTER FIVE

MELISSA
June 1985.

Jarrod laughs as he eats his dinner. 'You never stop talking lately. It's great you're getting on with the neighbours. I don't have to worry about you while I'm at work.'

I wipe my mouth with a napkin. 'You worry about me? Why?'

'I did when we first moved here. We'd gone from being around family all the time to our own home. With me being at work so much, I thought you'd be bored rattling around here on your own.'

I bristle and put my hand on the table, smoothing out the napkin. 'But I love our home. I like taking care of it and you.'

He puts his hand on mine. 'I know you do. But being here on your own day after day would have driven you mad eventually. I thought you might start saying you wanted a job.'

'No. I know how you feel about that. I'm happy to be provided for.'

'I just want to look after the old lady.'

I smack his arm. 'Hey, you. Less of the old. I'm only twenty.'

He slices through pie crust with his knife. 'How are the neighbours anyway? Any gossip?'

'Gaynor and Trevor are expecting,' I inform him.

His eyes widen. 'The older couple from the corner house? I thought they had grown up kids?'

'They do, and apparently, it's been a huge shock. Eighteen and nineteen their sons are. She thought she was in the menopause.'

'I'd get an abortion.'

My jaw drops. 'Jarrod. That's a life you're talking about.'

'What about their life? They start to get time to themselves and then it's back to nappies. Ugh.'

'I was hoping we'd be joining them soon,' I mumble quietly.

Jarrod pushes his plate away and rubs his belly. 'Let's just concentrate on filling my tum for now. A couple more years, Mel. When I can afford every possible thing you'll want and need. We're still only young.'

'Okay.' I take the dirty plates into the kitchen.

Jarrod comes up behind me and nibbles my neck. 'In the meantime, we can enjoy practising.'

He pulls my skirt up to my thighs and lowers my pants.

I put my hands on his. 'Jarrod, the neighbours will see.'

'No they won't.' He leans over and pulls down the blind. 'If any of them were looking they'll have to decide for themselves whether I'm helping you with the dishes or your knickers.'

'Jarrod!'

'I want you there, Mel. Let me love you there. Please?'

I close my eyes. I've only ever been with Jarrod and him with me. I'd been nervous when I'd given him his first blowjob when I was fourteen. When we had anal sex last year at nineteen, I was surprised to find I enjoyed it.

'Okay.'

He wets his finger and moves it around the entrance of my anus as if this will be adequate lubrication. Luckily for him, I like the feeling of roughness and invasion. I'd never tell him. I'd be nervous that he'd think I was a freak. He slowly pushes into my tight hole. I feel like he's going to rip me apart. His fingers come around the front and he strums across my clit. He plays me like a musical instrument. After all these years, he knows exactly what movement gets me to relax, and pushes further in.

'Oh, Mel. Fucking hell. You're so tight.'

'Love me, Jarrod. Please.'

He pushes me against the sink cabinet. Water from the front of the unit wets the waistband of my top. My long brown hair shakes forward with every thrust. He inserts a finger up my vagina and fucks me with it while he owns my back entrance.

He withdraws his finger and strums my clit so hard I don't know how his wrist doesn't snap. The friction builds. I reach under my top and cup my bare breasts in my hands. They're too small to need the restraint of a bra. I pinch my nipples as I head towards my crescendo.

'Now, God. Now, Mel.'

He thrusts so hard my waist is slammed into the

sink. I feel the warmth of his semen as he finishes. He withdraws straight away, grabbing some kitchen towel and wiping us both up.

'That is always worth coming home to. You know how to keep your man happy, Mel.'

I turn and smile as I reach up on my tiptoes to kiss his cheek. I didn't manage to come. I was so near, but as soon as he reached his orgasm, he left me behind. I feel like I want to go into the bathroom and fuck myself with my own fingers until I'm sore and replete. But I don't. I'd feel too embarrassed afterwards. Anyway, Jarrod is the only one I want to create my orgasms. He's all I've ever had and all I'll ever want.

'Tell me how it felt when I was inside you?'

He's always been so attentive to how he makes me feel. I describe in detail, embellishing my retelling with fictional details of my non-existent orgasm.

He's mine, and I'm his. It's how it's always been.

I follow him through into the lounge where he sits on the sofa, remote control in hand, flicking through TV channels.

'I was hoping to watch Brookside,' I tell him.

He switches it over to Channel Four. 'Be my guest, there's nothing on the other three channels.'

I lie on the sofa and put my feet across his knees. 'They're having a card game tonight. It's at Dave's.

Why don't you pop over there and get to know some of the blokes?'

Jarrod scratches his chin. 'I don't know.'

'Hey, what's up? Why are you so reluctant?'

He turns to me. 'They're all a few years older than me. A lot of them are family men and have jobs that require suits and stuff. I'd hate to think they judged me. Found me immature or stupid.'

'Jarrod,' I chastise him. 'They'll love you like I do. Go and see. You could be missing out on a great time.'

He chews on his lip, then moves my legs. 'Okay, I'll go. If they make me feel stupid, you have to promise to pee in their lemonade next time you're over there.'

I giggle. 'I promise.'

Jarrod has a great night. He starts making sure he can get home in time to join in their card and poker nights twice a week. We settle in, and life goes on. One night Jarrod comes home drunk, stating that it's time to start making babies.

I waited until he'd sobered up to quiz him. My heart thudded in my chest, an excitement fizzing deep within me. Hope he could extinguish just as quickly now he hadn't had a drink.

I walked into our bathroom where Jarrod was having a soak in the bath. 'Jarrod?'

'Yes, darling? Have you come to wash my back?'

I picked up the sponge and squirted some shower gel on it, lathering his back and around the nape of his neck where his light blonde hair reached midway.

'Did you mean what you said about starting a family?' I kept my voice light.

He grinned. 'Yes. The guys had a word with me last night. Well, Dave really. He said you can't wait forever. He's right. That man makes a lot of sense you know? I've saved quite a bit up now. I can stop working such long hours. We can get pregnant.' He winked at me. 'Then I can go out playing cards and poker while you change dirty nappies.'

I squeezed the sponge over his head so soap got in his eyes. He grabbed me in a split second and pulled me into the bath with him. The water splashed over the sides, and I feared for the lino and floorboards.

Jarrod kissed the tip of my nose.

'Get into bed. We should get started now.'

His wish was my command. It always had been.

By the end of the year, I was expecting our first child.

## CHAPTER SIX

### SAM
31 August 2014

I've opened the blind on the window so my therapist can see some daylight. Or rather can see me from his fixed viewpoint. I'm in my shorts and tee. They display my abs and glutes to perfection. As I dig the ground, he'll see my strength as my muscles cord with the push and pull of the spade. I'm digging a rectangle. For no reason other than to let him think I'm digging his grave. Psychology is the bomb. My house is an old miner's cottage. One house on its own, at the bottom of a country lane. There used to be others living here before the council bought them with the intent of developing the land. I planned to fight them, but they gave the idea up anyway, the land was deemed unsafe after a shaft collapsed on the old colliery. The other houses fell into ruin, but I looked after mine, even when I didn't live in it for a time.

I love it here. I'm a seven-minute walk away from the nearest house. I fixed a post-box at the end of the lane for any mail, so I'm left entirely alone. No one bothers to come all the way down here. Except children. Children and their enquiring minds. They come and play on Red Mountain. That's what they've named the red earth mounded into the hills surrounding my home; leftovers from Handforth's time as a mining community. I watch them sometimes as they climb up and then back down the hills, taking red dusted clothes back for their mothers to try to clean. They don't bother me. I have signs everywhere saying Beware of the Dogs. The children have assigned ghost stories to the row of abandoned-looking houses. I'm a wicked witch, and there's a curse on the rest of the row. The scrap cars piled up in the lot in the distance take their eye now and again, and they risk their lives to find a car they can make a den in. There's no fear when you're young and innocent.

I never look back at the room when I'm here, so I

don't know if he watches me dig, or thinks of his potential demise. I couldn't face the disappointment if he chose to ignore my efforts. It's better I remain unaware.

I cease digging and go to shower. I have another session with my therapist after lunch.

'I worked for Ed for a year. A whole year where I proved I was the best assistant ever. He could trust me with anything. I waited patiently for him to show me that trust. Sure enough, a test arose. Ed invited his boss, Mr Jacobs, to dinner at a city centre restaurant with a casino. He asked me to accompany them. Called it a business dinner. The invitation came with the words, "I hope I don't regret this." I knew then that I was on trial. To see if I was made of the same stuff he was. I remember that evening so well. I wore a long black chiffon dress that gathered at the waist and split up to the knee. When I sat, the material shifted to reveal a shapely calf, and gave Jacobs a hint of my black lace panties. I don't know what Ed slipped him during the evening, but come the time to gamble, Jacobs was like a racehorse that had thrown its rider. He blew money while attempting to get me to blow him. I'd smile and say let's bet again, the next one's bound to be a winner. But once again, Ed proved himself my superior. I was completely unaware that Mr Jacobs had a prior gambling addiction. Ed had purposely taken him to that restaurant and not revealed the casino attached until they'd had a few drinks. At which point, Jacobs had tried to leave. Then I'd shown up. Apparently, his ex-wife was a short-haired blonde.' I laugh.

'Something amusing?'

'Yes. I thought I'd been playing a great game until then - getting Ed to trust me. I knew my employment was based on my appearance, but I wasn't aware that I bore more than a passing resemblance to Jacobs' ex-wife. No wonder he employed me. It had nothing to do with my talents. But Ed knew why and made it part of a long game to destroy him.'

'How did that make you feel?'

'Like I was out of my league. I went home that night and smashed up my apartment. I'd been totally played. I felt like he'd won again.'

'Again?'

'Jacobs put a rope around his neck the following morning. When he didn't turn into work, I went to his home to apologise during my lunch break. I wanted to see if I could salvage anything. Maybe find a way to exact my revenge on Ed for using me. Instead, I saw his dangling feet when I peered through the letterbox.' I'm quiet for a moment as if paying my respects over again.

'After a couple of months, Ed was promoted to Jacobs' job.'

'That must have been frustrating?' The chains rattle, 'For fuck's sake, take these off!'

I stand up and lick my bottom lip. 'Still such venom after all these days. You really are impressive. That's why I had to do what I did next.' I sigh. 'You're not much use as a therapist, Ed. You're not designed for considering other people, are you? I think you need some time out to consider your outburst.'

'No, not again, please. We can sort this out. What do you want, Sam? Is it money? I have money. I'll give you money.'

I upturn my chair and throw it at the wall at the side of his head. He flinches.

'I don't want your money. I want you to take some responsibility for your actions. Your actions and your decisions have consequences. You don't even care. How many decisions have you made during your lifetime that have impacted on other people, huh? Have you given a thought to Jacobs' kids? How it felt to have a father who killed himself?'

'Oh, my God, are you Jacobs' daughter?' A ghost of a smile hints at Ed's lips.

'Of course not. I showed him my snatch, you sick

fuck. Stop trying to guess why I'm here and listen for once in your life.'

'I'll listen if you let me out of these cuffs.'

'You think you're unbreakable, Edward Bonham, and you still think you're in control. Open. Your. Eyes.'

I close the door on him and return to my digging. It's that or put the shovel into his skull, and that's not part of my plan.

## CHAPTER SEVEN

MELISSA
May 1986

I've been going around to Gaynor's a lot. Her son Andrew is now four months old.

'How did you decide on a name?' I ask her.

'Oh, we went through the baby name book and chose three each. We'd both picked Andrew. I'd picked it because of the royal wedding, but I didn't tell Trevor that, or it would have put him off. He doesn't believe in the royal family, thinks they're a waste for the taxpayer.'

I nod as if I know what she's talking about. I ignore politics and financial news. It's so deadly boring.

'So how are you feeling?' she asks me.

'Being pregnant is amazing.' I make a rubbing motion with the hand more or less permanently placed on my stomach. I'm showing now.

'You've been so lucky with no sickness.'

'I know. I've just been exhausted.'

'Make sure you rest. Get Jarrod to look after you.'

'Oh, he has.' I don't tell her how fussy he is, treating me like a delicate antique. He's so nervous about hurting the baby, and point blank refuses to make love while I'm pregnant. 'As soon as he gets home, he makes me put my feet up, and he won't let me lift anything.'

'Lucky bugger. Trevor just let me get on with it. Third child, all done twice before. You make the most of that special attention and get all the rest you can. Once that baby's here, you'll forget what sleep is.'

'I don't mind.' I reply. 'He or she will be worth it.'


I spend hours imagining who our child will resemble. Sometimes a boy who looks like his father, at other times a daughter with my dark-brown hair. I imagine she'll be beguiling and adorable, with huge chocolate brown eyes she'll peer through shyly while claiming her daddy's heart. I imagine us on shared shopping trips. We'll be able to have play-dates with Andrew, and Joanne before she starts nursery school. I visit the library and bring home several books on the subject of babies, careful to only choose light volumes, so I'm not carrying too much. I fill up on information, wanting to be as prepared as I can be. Jarrod laughs, saying you can't learn about babies from books. I have though. I know about feeding, winding, and how to bathe our baby. Literature is a joy and a wealth of information. My practical husband – who works with his hands – just doesn't see it; in my mind, I have several different scenarios of how and when to respond to our baby. I'll try them all until I get the best response. It's all in the research.

Over the last months, while I've been so tired, Jarrod has often met with one of the guys for a beer, or a card game. A new guy moved onto the estate at the beginning of the year. Edward. Jarrod says he's around the same age as us. He's an accountant. I sometimes watch him go to work from my bedroom window. He's a good-looking man. Tall. Walks very straight, as if there's a coat-hanger in his back. He and Jarrod hit it off. A fact that surprises me. They seem such opposites. A lot of the men's nights take place at Edward's home, as he doesn't have a wife to placate. Jarrod says Edward has told him he dates, but he wants to focus on his career.

## June 1986

I've become obsessed with watching Edward. He does everything with military precision. It's like he's a living robot. I think it's because I'm so bored. I'm getting quite large now, and I'm easily tired. I've become obsessed with people-watching, and Edward is by far the most interesting to spy on. Last weekend he had gardeners in. They fitted hedging. It is all uniform. The top of the hedge the same height all the way around. He waters his garden at ten pm every evening, even if the men are around playing a game of cards. They come out and drink their beer while he waters and they chat. At weekends, he heads off with his gym bag at nine am and doesn't return until twelve. Jarrod says he swims and then uses the weights. If he passes me in the street, he just nods his head. He's never actually spoken a word to me, and I want to know what his voice is like, the timbre of it.

It's Saturday, and he returned from the gym an hour ago. It's about time I properly spoke to him, given he's so close to Jarrod. Maybe I could invite him around for a meal one evening? After considering, I decide to ask him for some gardening advice. Wanting to look my best, I shower, dry my hair and use a scrunchie to tie it back into a ponytail. I've no need for makeup as my skin has a light glow from sitting in the garden in the sunshine, but I add a little Seventeen light pink lipstick, and I'm done. My sandals are next to the door, so I push my feet into them, noticing the tightness as the pregnancy has swollen them. Pulling the door closed behind me, I walk the three houses down to Edward's.

There's an open pathway to Edward's front door. Plain brown curtains hang at the windows. Net curtains ensure you can't see in. The door is painted an emerald green, which blends in with the garden. It's boring. I'd expect Edward to have a striking house, given his exactness. I press the doorbell and hear its buzz. Net curtains are pulled aside, then I hear the chain removed and the door opens.

I look up. My mouth drops. Up close, Edward is exotic looking. His skin is tanned from the sun and golden-brown. He looks almost apache Indian. His neck is thick, and I wonder what size collar his shirts are.

'Can I help you?'

His voice is deep like it comes from the earth itself. Commanding. I expect winds to swirl as he speaks. He has an unearthly presence like he's some kind of a god. I'm fascinated by his aura.

'Are you okay, Mrs Simmons?'

I jolt. 'Sorry. Pregnancy brain.' I pat my stomach as if he can't see the significant bump protruding from below my bust. 'I'm sorry to bother you, but I wondered if you could tell me if there's anything you're feeding your hedges? They are well, fantastic looking and ours, well...' I peer over my shoulder to my own house where our hedge is uneven and full of half-dead, brown twigs.

'You're taking a keen interest in gardening now?' He raises an eyebrow. 'I would have thought you had lots of preparations to do for the baby.'

His tone is flat and cold. Suddenly I don't want to be here. I feel foolish. He is looking at me as if he knows full well that I have no interest in gardening.

'I'm prepared for my baby, but I'm becoming restless and need something to do.' I reply, my voice running out of steam by the end of the sentence. Why did I come here? I should just go. I turn away.

'Other than sitting in the window watching people? Wait there. I've just bought a new packet of feed. I'll get it for you. I can buy another.' He closes the door, gently, but still in my face. I wait, though right now I want the ground to swallow me up. *This man is around the same age as you*, I tell myself. *Why are you so intimidated?* I straighten my shoulders as the door opens again.

'There you are. Instructions are on the packet. Follow them precisely. Will that be all?'

I note the name of the product. 'Thank you, but I'm perfectly capable of buying my own feed. I won't need to inconvenience you by taking yours.' I keep my hands firmly by my sides, not taking the offered item. 'Good day, Mr Bonham. I appreciate your time.'

A hint of a smile appears. 'Call me Edward,' he says.

'I doubt I'll need to call on you again at all, Mr Bonham.'

I walk away, trying to salvage what remains of my dignity. The man is awful. I don't want Jarrod around him.

July 1986

. . .

From then on, when I pass Edward in the street he nods his head and says a curt, "Mrs Simmons". On one occasion, he passes as I am coming out of my house. He looks at the still messy hedges and raises an eyebrow before continuing down the street. My fascination with him turns into hatred, the hormones from my pregnancy no doubt fuelling what would ordinarily be an annoyance.

It's a Wednesday evening when Jarrod once again leaves me to play cards. I'm seven and a half months pregnant, feeling fabulous, and like I want to have sex with my husband.

'Oh, do you have to go around there tonight? I was hoping we could have a night in.' I smile in what I hope is a teasing fashion.

Jarrod pulls me towards him and kisses the top of my head. 'You know I'm not doing anything to risk that baby.' He strokes my stomach.

'You're always out with the guys.' I pout.

Jarrod laughs. He strokes his chin. 'You were the one who said I had no friends and needed to go out with them. Now you want me at home. Those hormones really do mess with a woman.'

A flash of anger crosses my face.

'Whoa, with that glare I'm out of here.' He dashes to the door and almost flings himself through it in his haste.

I throw myself down on the sofa, completely bored. There's nothing to do but watch a television programme until I fall asleep.

I come to wondering where I am. The side of my face is crushed into the arm of the sofa. Drool runs from the corner of my lip. I glance at the clock. It's after one am. I presume Jarrod went straight upstairs so as not to disturb me and after coming around for a minute or two I walk upstairs to the bedroom. He's not there. The bed covers are completely untouched. I run back downstairs. Jarrod is always back by midnight. My anger rises to the surface. Where the fuck is he? I stroll into the kitchen to get a glass of water. My mouth is dry from being asleep and it needs to be well lubricated for when he does get home and I give him a piece of my mind. I raise the blind and peer at Edward's house. There's no sign of anyone on the street. From the corner of my eye, I notice movement. Sandra is waving to me from her window and indicating I should come outside.

I walk out of the front door to meet her.

'They're late, aren't they? What are you still doing up? You should be resting that baby.'

'I fell asleep on the sofa. Shall we collect our husbands? It's that bloody Edward. He's leading them astray.'

Sandra laughs, 'They've probably passed out on his sofa.' She looks back at her house. 'I'll lock up. The kids will be okay for a few minutes, won't they?'

'We're only going three doors down. You can see your house from there. Don't let me go there alone. Jarrod will complain I'm embarrassing him, whereas if we both turn up, we can appear like overbearing wives together.'

'Okay. Let me lock the door.'

As we walk down Edward's path, there's jazz music coming from the house. Subdued lighting comes through the net curtain.

I knock on the door, but there's no answer.

I tut and turn towards Sandra.

'What shall we do now?' she asks.

'You can see a bit under the net curtain.'

Sandra looks at me with a raised eyebrow.

'I snooped a while back, so shoot me.' I laugh. 'It would seem I'm a nosy neighbour.' I wander to the front and bend to peer underneath. I feel the weight of my bump as I get into this uncomfortable position.

Jarrod lies on the floor. It takes me a while to process the fact that his lips are locked with another man's. That the other man, Edward, is fucking my husband up his backside. I can just make out small grunts accompanying the loud jazz music. Dave is passed out in a chair. I turn away and throw up in the garden.

Sandra rushes over. 'Mel, whatever is the matter?'

I point.

She looks through the curtains herself. Her scream rings out into the quiet of the street.

My thoughts rush at me. They'll know we're here now. I need to get away. If I run back to my own home, maybe I can pretend I've never seen this. Go back to my settled, normal life.

But Sandra is in front of me, battering on the window.

'Stop it.' I grab hold of her arms. 'We need to get out of here. Then decide what we will do.'

She nods. 'I'm going back to my babies.'

She runs towards her house. I attempt to run after her though with my pregnancy I'm not fast. A stitch starts in my side, and I pause in the middle of the street, rubbing my stomach. Edward's front door opens, and Dave dashes through it. Jarrod stands in the doorway watching Dave but avoiding my gaze.

It's this distraction that means I'm in the middle of the road when the taxi comes around the corner, hitting me sideways on. No one would expect a woman to be standing in the middle of the road of a quiet cul-de-sac at one-thirty am I'm sure.

The world goes black.

# CHAPTER EIGHT

MELISSA
January 1987

When a car collides with the side of a pedestrian, the impact to the lower body means that the lower half accelerates while the top stays relatively still. The body then wraps around the front of the vehicle, in my case, causing my head to hit the windshield, tearing my face in the process. The resultant fall to the ground causes my skull to fracture. The taxi will have a dent in the hood and a smashed windshield. This will be recorded by the insurance companies, along with the burnt tyre marks on the road from braking. It's the braking that caused my injuries, although not braking would have been far worse.

I watch *St. Elsewhere* these days and consider this is what it must have been like on scene and in the hospital. Shining lights in my eyes to check pupil responses. Listening to my chest, hearing the diminished breathing caused by the diaphragmatic rupture. You kind of need the muscle that runs across the bottom of your ribcage to breathe. Blunt trauma creates a whole host of problems.

Losing a lot of blood sends a body into hypovolaemia. When this happens, it tries to save blood. My body considered my unborn baby to be non-essential to my survival and stopped the blood running to my uterus, diverting it elsewhere. If the car impact hadn't already caused the death of my daughter, then my own body would have killed her instead. It's a sobering thought and not one a mother wants to dwell on. My womb and my dead child are removed from my body. I do not get to cradle her because I am unconscious.

Torn knee ligaments, lacerations, abrasions.

I spend time in the intensive care unit as they wait to see if I'll live. I'm moved to the high dependency unit. Then to a general ward where I'm given physiotherapy. Finally, I'm allowed home.

Home.

After several months in hospital, I'm unsure of what to expect when I get there.

I know what not to expect.

My husband.

I lost him the night of my accident. He ceased to exist, just like our daughter. I was abandoned without a second thought, no explanation, nothing.

From that day, I distract myself from my thoughts every time he comes to my mind.

My parents open the door. The house belongs to me now. It's clean. My mother has obviously been through it with stealth. My house is stocked with groceries. A vase of flowers sits on the table. As soon as they leave, I throw them in the bin; they remind me of my days in hospital. I never want to see a flower in a vase again. Later, I gaze out of the window and stare across at Sandra and Dave's. I wonder how they went on. If they are still together. Then I look at Edward's.

Later, there's a knock on the door. A glimpse through the peephole reveals Dave. His hair is greyer; he looks ten years older than the last time I saw him.

I open the door, slowly. I'm unsure if I want to open it at all.

'Dave.'

'Can I come in?'

I pause before opening the door and indicating that he should enter.

Dave is a tall bloke, and he seems too large for my living room. I can't help but think about the last time I saw him. I mustn't let these thoughts in.

'How is Sandra?' I ask.

'That's why I'm here,' he says. His eyes close, tears on his lashes.

I don't want him to speak. I don't want to know what that tone of voice means. That given up, reluctant tone.

'She blamed herself for you being in the road. She'd look at the kids and say it wasn't fair that she had two daughters and you'd lost yours. She couldn't look at me either. She wouldn't believe I hadn't taken part. I didn't know, Mel, I swear.'

'How did she...?'

'She took an overdose.'

'When?'

'A month after the accident.'

I stand still though I don't know how. 'I'm sorry for your loss, but I'd like to be alone now.'

He nods and walks towards the door.

'Is he still here?' I ask.

'Yes.' Then he updates me.

Edward now lives with his girlfriend, Inez. While we all suffered, Edward moved on.

Damage to the brain after an accident can sometimes leave a person suffering from behavioural problems. It can be like they are two different people, Jekyll and Hyde if you will. I like to blame my accident, but I had issues with Mr Bonham from the get go. The man is inhuman. I vow that one day I will get that man to show some emotion. To apologise for the actions that resulted in my loss. But for now, I am too damaged, too broken and I hole up behind the walls of my home and try to survive each day.

Dave and I become close. We cling to each other, with the shared history of that evening. The first time Dave kisses me, I let him. He's a decent looking bloke, but I don't think I'm capable of love anymore, there's not much room beyond the hatred I keep deep within. I realise however that I can become a mother to Becky and Joanne. Babies I never gave birth to but can love as my own. Dave wants to move, but I insist we stay in his family home. I tell him the children need that stability. We get married. One thing I discover is sex is something that can be loving one minute and like animals attacking each other the next. I realise what a pathetic lover Jarrod was and that the right lover can make your body sing to the heavens. I crave Dave's contact, even if I struggle to sum up my feelings for him. With the girls, I try my best to show good and positive emotions. Our life together, bearing in mind our past, is a good one. But the hatred simmers beneath me like a pilot light, kept on, waiting to be turned up. I tell Dave the truth from the beginning of our relationship. That one day I will make them pay. He hates them as much as I do. He says he'd help me, but I'm not sure I'd let him.

After I moved into Dave's, I sold my own home and put the proceeds in a bank account, telling Dave my parents were struggling financially and I'd given them a loan. I learnt to type, and as the children got older, I began work as a medical secretary to a surgeon. Dave refused to take any money from me towards the household bills, telling me to spend it on myself or the kids. I bank my salary too. My parents pass away. I keep the home we moved to when I was fifteen, but I save the money from their investments. All saved. For what at that point in time I didn't know. But there, in case I should need it.

All the while Edward lives across the street with Inez. Inez with her long dark hair, gleaming white teeth and legs up to her armpits. They never even glance towards me or Dave. It's like they live in another world. They taunt me with their blandness. I wonder what they are like behind closed doors. The house remains the same from the outside. The same uniformity. Edward's routine never changes, despite now having his partner living with him. Turn your thoughts off, I tell myself. One day, but not now. A man like Edward considers everything. The fact that I do nothing will hopefully taunt him as he will expect my next move at any moment.

However, I let the years' pass. Because when I'm ready, I need to have nothing to lose.

## CHAPTER NINE

SAM

1 September 2014

I take Edward puzzles. Sudoku, crosswords, anagrams. Sometimes I sit and watch him while he does them. He can solve an anagram at a rapid pace. His intellect is sharp. That's what I want. I don't need him going into a confused state while he's here. I want him to know exactly what is happening. I want him to figure out this puzzle. Who I am and why he is here.

'I have a new treat for you today, Edward. A new puzzle. Let's see if you can figure this one out.'

I make sure his other hand remains restrained, and I am clear to do my work.

I bring out the shaver and shave the hair on his chest.

Edward blanks his face and pretends I'm not touching him. I sweep over his skin with a towel and rub him down with alcohol wipes. I love the smell, so strong like they mean business. I breathe it in. Then I get my pens. Slowly I outline the letter M all over his chest. As I do, I say it. 'M. M. M. M. M.' This gets his attention. 'What?' I ask. After a flash of annoyance crosses his features, no doubt directed at himself, he goes blank-faced again. I leave a decent space after the M as there are more letters to go there, four in total. 'I.I.I.I.' 'N.N.N.N.N.N.' 'E.E.E.E.E.' I laugh. 'E.E.E. That'll be the sound you might be making in a minute.' I outline the same letters on his back.

Nothing. The blank face remains.

While you are tattooing, good hand-eye coordination is required. However, the main talent is attention to detail. My purest trait. Attention to every single possible detail. I am completely focused on the tasks I need to execute.

My tattoo machine is one of the best you can buy. The best equipment for the best tattoos. Metal tubes.

No disposables for me. Then I begin. I work solidly for two hours. This sounds like a lot, but when taking care, it means just a small amount of the body is now covered with permanent letters. I'll do this daily until my project is complete. I've almost done with Edward now, to be honest. I wrap his abdomen in cling film. I'll come back and wash my work with warm soapy water in a few hours and blot it. I need to make sure there's no chance of infection.

Adrenaline will be coursing through Edward's body now. I get up to leave him, and he gives me the filthiest look I've received so far. Apart from a tightening of his jaw, he remained impassive throughout my work. His strength is admirable, but it just makes me want to break him more.

'I have no idea what you are trying to achieve, but this smacks of desperation.'

I smile at him.

'Yet I know your body has always been a temple to you, where you can worship that god you follow. You know, yourself. Now when you look in the mirror, you'll always think of me.'

'You flatter yourself.'

'I'm pleased with my work. I am a fucking brilliant tattooist. I have you to thank for that, Edward. Had you not put me on the path I found myself on, I may never have learnt, and I was a natural. That's what my teacher said. It's really hard to get an apprenticeship, but I was that damn good.'

'Who are you?'

'Oh dear, Edward. Is it so hard to work out?'

'I don't understand your puzzles. Just tell me who you are and what you want.'

I smirk. 'What if I said that when I knew you my name was Melissa Simmons?'

Edward's eyes widen, and his jaw slackens. 'Don't be ridiculous.'

'Why is that ridiculous?'

'Melissa is decades older than you. Brunette. Different eye colour. I don't know who you are, but you are not Melissa Simmons.'

I sit back in my chair and cross my legs. This time my smile is genuine. A great big beam across my face. Then I talk. 'I'd better explain the puzzle that you aren't getting, Ed. Let's give you an anagram. Your clue: Sam lies. Have you worked it out yet? Melissa. Get it? Rearrange the letters of Sam lies. Yes, I fucking well do.'

Ed rattles his chain, trying to get away from the wall. Finally, I have the reaction I've been looking for.

'You're lying. You have to be. Who are you and what do you want?'

'All in good time, Edward. I'm bored now.'

I close the door on him and tidy my equipment away ready for tomorrow.

# CHAPTER TEN

MELISSA
June 2000

Dave always knew the day would come. At twenty, and sixteen years of age, our daughters were old enough to deal with my leaving. Becky had a child of her own now, and Dave doted on his grandson. I wanted to. I made it look as if I thought Jude was the cutest grandchild ever, but in truth, I was restless.

I had to win.

So, I left.

. . .

My travels took me to Suffolk, a place of childhood holidays. I recalled seeing the heavily tattooed punks from the shop on the sea front - my parents dragging me along when I wanted to peer in and see the permanent artwork being etched on people's bodies. My mother tutted at my interest and declared that they'd regret it when they were older. When they were sixty and had a past boyfriend/girlfriend's name on their arm. The tattoo shop was still there to my utter delight. Tattoo Heaven. I walked in and asked to be an apprentice. Bobby, the owner, took one look at my appearance - a thirty-five-year-old woman with medium length dark brown hair, perfectly manicured hands and Clarks shoes on my feet and he guffawed. He made me a coffee, and I never looked back. He had nothing to lose. I didn't need a wage, and I was a quick learner. I'd adored art at school and took to my new profession like a brick takes to cement. I built a firm foundation in a new career and developed a friendship that would last for years. Bobby told me he had no intention of settling down with one woman. There was too much pussy on offer, especially the babes who loved getting tats and hanging around the parlour. I moved in with him, rented a room in his house. It didn't bother me hearing him banging his whores. I stayed there for three years.

Bobby knew everything, and he understood when it was time for me to move on.

'I'm here when you're ready for the next step. I'll help you all the way, you know that.'

'I know.'

'I love you like a sister. Going to miss seeing your face around here though.'

'Trade will be affected by the loss of one of your star tattooists.' I snorted.

'You're joking, but it's true. There's always a place for you here, Mel. Always.'

'I won't be the same when I return.'

Bobby shakes his head. 'You'll always be you, but like our customers, with a few modifications.'


From Suffolk, I travelled to New York. Now thirty-eight, I was more than ready to experience more of life. It was time for the scars of my past to heal. The ones on my body from the car accident had faded, but I made an appointment with a plastic surgeon. My years working as a medical secretary for a surgeon had prepared me for what lay ahead. After several consultations, the surgeon began the work of clearing my body of its scars. I lived as a New Yorker, soaking up the best places on earth, while I continued with surgery. I attended dramatic arts classes, learning how to speak in different tones and accents, and became a total gym bunny. I often ran around Central Park when I wasn't recovering from surgery. I had my hair cropped short and dyed blonde. I had a facelift, breast augmentation, a butt-lift. The fake tan took my pale skin away, and contacts turned my brown eyes blue. Living on salads and fruit, my skin became youthful and glossy. The process took years, during which, I kept in touch with Bobby and Dave, though I never sent photographs or anything in writing that could fall into the wrong hands. Dave kept me informed about Edward and Inez. Edward was becoming a big name at the accountancy firm he'd moved to after "the incident". They still appeared happy.

I got theatre work. It didn't pay much, but I got to be other people for months on end. It suited me. I never formed a relationship with another male. In fact, my feelings for Dave surprised me. It took leaving him for me to realise how important he was to me. I really did love him. However, I couldn't explore that while I was still so consumed by hatred. I tell Dave to move on, but not to tell me if he meets someone else. It would hurt too much. But my love for him is not strong enough to take me home. I hate, more than I love.

It's 2013 when I finally decide it's time to go home. To finish what I started so I can live the rest of my life.

I don't tell Dave I'm home. But Bobby is there when I need him. He stays in my apartment when required. He's a good friend, but the offer of money makes him a better one.

Now another person is dead because of Edward Bonham, and I've had enough. He needs to be held accountable for his actions.

There's no sign of Melissa Simmons, nee Jones. I'm Sam Briers now – Edward Bonham's right-hand lady. I've to move on from what happened to Mr Jacobs. Regroup, and figure my next steps.

It's ridiculously easy to purchase fake documents. Bobby saw to all of that for me. My CV and references are perfect for the personal assistant role. What I didn't expect was silence from Ed. Other than asking me to work, he barely addressed me at all. From my time working in the tattoo parlour to my time in theatre, I'd experienced nothing but noise. Bobby would always have music thrashing through speakers while customers chatted and equipment whirred. For the theatre, I'd learn my lines in peace, but practice and productions were always frantic.

I'd speak to Kerry in the staff room, but Ed didn't like idle office chatter. He'd give me plenty of work as if challenging me to not to be able to complete it. I did. Even if it meant staying late, that work was always done. We became a productive team despite the lack of friendly communication between us. I learnt all about his customers, and his business. Unfortunately, there were no skeletons. I'd quizzed Kerry, but any rumours about Ed seemed to be just that, rumours – no doubt made up by staff who couldn't get a real story on him.

As the year went on, I began to see no reason to keep working for him. I'd uncovered nothing in terms of exacting revenge. Then one day he went out to the bathroom, leaving his suit jacket on the back of his chair. As quickly as I could, I ransacked his pockets, looking for anything I could use. There was a thin, black address book. I flicked through it, my heart beating fast in my chest, my hands wavering. If he caught me, I was fucked. There was nothing of interest in the pages but in a pocket at the back was a photo of Ed in a Scout uniform. I noted the scout group then shoved his address book back in his pocket and dashed back to my desk.

When Ed walked back, he appraised me. 'Your face is very flushed, Miss Briers. What have you been doing while I was gone?'

'I'm, well, I'm handing in my notice, Ed.'

He stops moving. 'Sorry? Is there a problem?'

'No. I feel it's time for me to move on. Obviously, I'll work a month's notice, but this job isn't for me.'

'You're extremely efficient. You've been a real asset,' he says, a frown appearing on his brow. 'I hope I haven't done anything to offend you. I know I can seem cold at times.'

'No. It's the job. It's too quiet. I can't sit there every day with lots of work but no one to talk to. It's not me. You need an assistant like yourself.'

'Well, what sort of thing did you want to do?'

'Normal assistants would arrange meetings for you. Take messages from your wife. That sort of thing. You handle all your own phone calls, and well, I'm bored.'

'But you have plenty of work.'

'Paperwork yes, but nothing else. I'm going crazy. I live alone and basically work alone. I need more excitement in my day.'

Ed scratched his chin. 'So, if I give over more responsibility to you. Let you take the phone calls, arrange my diary, etc., you'll stay?'

'I'd give it a try.'

'Fine. Stay, and we'll try working your way. This isn't going to be easy for me. I abhor change, and I don't like to not be in control. You'd better not mess up.'

'I won't. Thank you.'

The first time I speak to his wife on the phone, a tingle shoots up my spine. At last, a way in.

'Hello. Is that Ed's Assistant?'

'It is.'

'Hi, I'm his wife, Inez.' It's said in a friendly voice but with an underlying tone of suspicion. I suppose I'd be suspicious if instead of getting through to my husband I suddenly got his assistant. I'm being viewed as a threat, and I love it.

'Good morning, Mrs Bonham,' I reply, making her sound her middle-age. 'Ed's out at a meeting. Can I take a message for you?'

'That's very kind, but I'll try his mobile.'

'Okay then. Well, it was very nice to speak to you, Mrs Bonham.'

'Please, call me Inez.'

'Okay, well I'm Sam. Sam Briers.'

'I know. Good day, Sam, I'm sure we'll speak again soon.'

The phone call ends.

. . .

Later in the month, there's a boring annual business meeting followed by a business dinner. Wives are invited, and the thought of seeing Inez while I'm in my new body makes me sweat. All staff members are expected to attend, but I didn't want to meet her under these circumstances. I needn't have worried. Ed informs me that he keeps his wife and personal life entirely separate from his business affairs.

I sit beside him at the meal. I wear a corporate black trouser suit with a grey silk blouse. Edward asks about everyone else's families while giving cursory replies about his own.

'Do you know I've only ever seen photos of his wife?' Jack Simpson bellows, slightly inebriated. 'Never met her. I don't think she exists. Either that or he's nipped to Thailand and bought one. Sure she ain't a ladyboy, Ed?'

Only I notice the clench of his jaw.

'I've met her,' I say. Ed looks at me, believing that I'm lying. 'And spoken to her many times on the phone. She seems lovely.'

'Oh, right,' Jack says subdued. I notice his wife has a tight pinch to her mouth and is obviously embarrassed about her husband's behaviour.

The rest of the meal passes quietly. At the end of

the evening, corporate photographs are taken to be displayed on the office walls.

When Jack returns to work on Monday morning, he has a black eye and a split lip. He gives the story of having been mugged while leaving the party. His inebriation making him a target, while his wife waited in the car.

But I watch Ed stretch his hand out several times that day as if his knuckles are sore. Though there's no evidence of bruising, his skin tone masks any darkened areas.

It's become my aim to cause as much trouble between Ed and his wife as I can. I begin by sending a copy of the corporate photo through the post. In it, I'm standing at the side of Ed smiling at him. Inez can see that her husband's assistant is a slim blonde.

The calls to the office to check on her husband's whereabouts increase.

I make my tone friendly when she calls.

'Hi, Inez. No, he's not here. Gone to yet another meeting. I don't know what they find to talk about. Hardly ever see him these days.'

I hear the panic in her voice, a slight tremble to the tone. 'Can you get him to call me when he's back? He's not answering his mobile.'

'I will do.'

He's not answering his mobile because I knocked it onto silent earlier when it was on my desk. She can ring and ring, and he'll not know until he checks it.

Another time I put the answerphone on to say we're both at lunch. We are, separately, but Inez leaves a further message for her husband to ring her.

I know something's amiss when Ed's daily meditation runs over and I'm still waiting outside his office door at eight forty-five am.

Finally, he opens his door and asks me to come in.

His face is drawn. He doesn't look like he's slept well. He has a couple of creases in his jacket and a scratch on his left cheek.

He watches me appraise him, but says nothing.

'I'm sorry, Sam,' he tells me. 'But I'm going to have to ask you be transferred. It's my wife. She's very possessive, and well, she believes there's something going on between us.'

'But that's stupid. Do you want me to talk to her?'

He shakes his head. 'No. My wife has some issues. I don't wish to discuss them, but there's a reason she's like she is. I can write you a marvellous reference anytime, Sam, but from tomorrow you'll be working for one of the other accountants.'

'No. I quit, and I'm going off sick so as not to work any notice.'

'Why leave secure employment?'

'I've another job lined up. I was going to tell you.'

I can see he doesn't believe me. I can also see he doesn't care one way or another. His mind is on his wife.

Finally, I got through the mask and found his weakness.

Her.

## CHAPTER ELEVEN

### SAM/SELMA
June 2014

I can now focus completely on Inez Bonham.

I visit a top hairdresser's in London and have cherry red hair extensions. Filler gives me a plumper mouth. My eyebrows are darkened and my eyelashes tinted. I change my contacts to a pale grey and wear a lot of makeup and boho style clothing. I'm now Selma.

Bobby delights in the fact that I finally want a tattoo of my own. He tattoos a dreamcatcher on my upper left arm. I fully intend to catch Inez Bonham's dreams and turn them into nightmares.

Every single morning Inez walks her dog, a pathetic looking chihuahua, to a cafe where she stays for a drink. On this particular morning, Bobby rushes towards her, pinches the dog, and dashes off. Inez screams, her surrogate child stolen. I use my gym-honed body, dressed in a bright floral loose tee and tight pale blue jogging pants, and tear after the "thief". I snatch the dog back, and Bobby runs away as planned.

I jog back to her and return her dog. 'Here. You okay?'

Inez weeps. She's taller than me, and tall for a woman at six feet to my five foot five. She's always walked hunched over, afraid to own her height. Her long brown hair reminds me of my own when I was Melissa. Her passing resemblance to me makes me so angry I have to clench my hands behind my back, else I may attempt to rip her hair away and scratch at her face. I focus on my breathing. *Calm down, talk to her.*

My accent is now scouse. I adore playing these new roles. I was always supporting cast in the plays, now I'm centre stage.

'I... Oh, my God. He stole Bounty. She's my baby. Shit. Should I call the police?' she asks.

'There's no point. He was obviously an opportunist and is long gone. Waste of time. Listen, there's a nice cafe near here that takes dogs. Can I buy you a hot drink? I'd like to make sure you're okay before I leave you.'

She clutches my arm in a strong grip. 'Thank you so much for rescuing her. Yes, I think I will have a nice cup of tea with some sugar for the shock.'

'Let's head to Cafe Coco then. It's this way.' I indicate up the street.

'Oh, I know, I go there every day. That's where I was heading to. I don't think I've seen you there before?'

I smile. 'I only moved to this area last week. First thing I did was find a great place to have coffee. It's a priority you know? I can't survive without it.'

'I know what you mean. Coco's has become part of my daily routine. My husband works long hours, and I get a little bored.'

'Mine too.' I twist the wedding band on my left hand. 'He's a self-employed writer. We travel a lot as it depends on where he sets his next novel. For some reason, he chose Rotherleigh for his latest, so here we are.'

'Wow, that sounds so exciting,' she says.

We reach the doorway of the cafe, step inside, and take a seat. She sits Bounty in a basket on one of the chairs, and it stays there, its face vacant. I can't understand the fascination for these toy dogs. They look like they could break apart should you blow on them.

'So why the name Bounty?' I ask. Though the answer is pathetic and obvious.

'Because my little sweetie girl is brown with a white belly. She made me think of the chocolate bar.' She tickles the dog's belly. It still does nothing.

'Do you dress her up? I know a lot of small breed owners do that?'

'Oh, yes,' she tells me, her shock wearing off as she becomes enthused. 'She has little jumpers, pyjamas, the lot. Basically, she's like my baby substitute.' Her face falls.

'I can't have children,' I confide.

'You can't? I'm so sorry. Neither can I, and we've tried to adopt, but that hasn't happened either. So, Bounty is my baby.' She looks at me. 'I sound pathetic, don't I?'

'No, you don't. You've done more than I have. To be honest, I block out the fact I can't have children.' I smile and take a deep breath. 'I can't believe I'm telling you all this when we've only just met. I'm usually so private.'

'Me too,' Inez agrees. 'My husband is an extremely private man and likes me to be the same. He's always preferred it to be just me and him, and well, it can be difficult to make friends, you know?'

'I do. Well, all you needed was to get your dog almost kidnapped, and now you have one. If you want one that is? Maybe we could just meet here occasionally for a hot drink?'

'That would be lovely,' Inez says. 'Some female adult conversation. I'm here almost every morning. Same time, ten until around eleven. Any time you want to come along, feel free.'

'You might regret that invitation when I turn up every day because I'm bored.'

'No I won't,' Inez says. 'You're the first genuine person I've met in a long time. I could use a friend and, well, I'm sorry about your child situation, but it's nice to have someone who understands if you see what I mean.'

'I do. So, what will your husband say about you having a new friend?'

Inez chews on her lip. 'I'm not going to tell him. He'd want to meet you, and he can be rather aloof. He might scare you away. I'm going to keep you all for myself.'

'Fine by me. I'll not tell my husband either. We'll be secret best friends forever.'

Inez giggles. She looks so fucking ugly when she does so.

I take a sip of my latte. I can't stand milk, but Selma drinks it.

'Oh, my God, I haven't even asked your name, and I'm saying we need to be BFFs.' I put a hand over my mouth.

'I'm Inez,' she says.

'Selma.' I hold out my hand, and she shakes it. Her hand in mine makes me want to heave. 'Inez is a beautiful name. Very unusual for around here I would think.'

'Yes. My name was given to me with love. I adore it.' She smiles. I want to stick the end of my spoon in her eyeball. 'Selma is unusual too.'

'My mother always was a bit dramatic. She wanted to call me Thelma after the film *Thelma and Louise*, but my father ruled it out, so Selma it was,' I lie. I don't know how I make this shit up. I hope she doesn't check the film release date as I've no fucking idea if the timeline matches up with my story. I berate myself for being careless.

I finish up my drink. 'Well, I'd better go and get my housework done. That's the deal for me being a stay at home housewife. I keep the place clean. And believe me, when my other half's writing it's needed. He loads up on mugs and dirty plates. I don't see him for days. He's like a hermit. In fact, I end up smelling him before I see him.' I laugh.

'Mine works long hours. I get really bored on my own, but he leaves me a list of things to do while he's out.'

'Sounds very bossy.'

'He likes order and routine. Mess displeases him. He's a believer that a woman's place is in the home.'

I guffaw. 'Oh, my God. I couldn't live with someone like that. I'd rebel.'

Inez's face falls.

'Gosh, I'm sorry. That was insensitive of me.'

'No, it's okay. I like his order. It makes me feel safe.'

'Why would you not feel safe?' I put a look of mock concern on my face.

'Oh. Forget that. Daft turn of phrase. I can get a little agoraphobic. Hide away. That's why I have the dog and go out for coffee every morning. I'd be tempted to never go out otherwise.'

I stand up and lean over Inez and give her a hug. Then I tickle the zombie dog's ears.

'Well, I'll probably see you in the morning. If you're sure that's okay with you?'

She smiles. 'I'm already looking forward to it.'

I walk out of the cafe and walk back to my apartment. When I'm safely inside, I rush to the bathroom where I vomit up the drink I had. My body shakes with pent up emotion. I lie on my bed and let the thoughts of the morning swirl around my mind. When I feel calmer, I take out my journal and write down our entire conversation and my observations. I don't want to forget anything that I can use in the future.

Then I drink some water and eat an apple before firing up the computer to plan my next move.

## CHAPTER TWELVE

### SELMA
August 2014

From here on in it's a breeze. We meet most days at the coffee shop. She's so desperate for a friend. To be liked. It's tragic.

From the copy I'd made of Ed's electronic diary before I left the accountants, I know he's due to attend a conference in London today and will be staying there for a further two days. When Inez brings it up at the coffee shop, I try hard not to smirk.

'My husband's away for a couple of days on business. Would you want to-' Her voice fades.

'Want to what? Go to the cinema maybe?'

'Erm, no, actually, I wondered if you'd like to come over to the house? I could make a meal. That's if you aren't busy with your husband.'

'No, I'd love to. He's in his writing cave for a change. I'm climbing the walls with nothing to do. He hasn't come to bed the last two days, he's slept in his chair.'

'Well, you could stay if you like? That way you could drink. We could have a girly sleepover. I never did that when I was younger.'

'No girly sleepovers? How come? They're a rite of passage. Midnight feasts and chick flicks.'

'I wasn't allowed.'

'Well then, I'm definitely staying over, and I'll bring films and nail polish.'

She smiles. 'I think for the first time ever I might actually be pleased my husband has to stay away.'


Inez lets me into the house. The outside is as uniform as it was all those years ago, but there are no longer net curtains, modern times have ditched that look. Instead, there are blinds, angled so as not to be able to see inside. The house is surprisingly masculine. All greys and sharp angled furniture. I thought Inez would have let herself free with decorating, but it seems her husband's control is in the decor too.

Bounty comes yapping at my feet. I want to swing my leg and kick her into the wall. She must sense it as she nips my ankle.

'Ow.'

'Bounty. Naughty girl, come here.'

I watch as Bounty is fed three pieces of steak. Well, talk about rewarding bad behaviour. *Don't worry, Bounty, I'll give you a treat later too.*

Inez cooks an amazing meal. To be frank, I'm astounded by her culinary skills.

'I watch a lot of cookery programmes,' she explains, 'and then I practice the recipes. I have nothing but time.'

'I quite like a good cookery programme too,' I tell her.

'We are so alike. I can't believe it,' says Inez. 'Do you like the film *Chocolate*?'

'Do I? Johnny Depp plus chocolate? What's not to like?' I laugh.

'I wasn't sure you'd have seen it, with you being so young.'

Fuck. I forget I'm only supposed to be in my twenties.

'Well it's a classic, isn't it?'

She leans back against the sofa and sighs. 'I don't know why you want to hang around with a middle-aged woman like me and not someone your own age.' Her face falls.

'Why? How old are you?' I ask as if I don't already know.

'I'm almost forty-nine.'

'Wow. You don't look it,' I lie. 'I thought you were early forties.'

'How old are you? If you don't mind me asking, that is?'

'Twenty-seven,' I tell her. 'Age is just a number, Inez. I don't make friends based on it. Most women my age are having babies, and well, you know what that subject does for me. I'd rather hang with you. You have life experience, history. We have lots to chat about. I bet you've done some amazing things in your life.'

I see a wobble to her lip. A nervous tremor to her hand. 'My life's been quite stale,' she lies.

It doesn't matter. I know all her secrets anyway, whether she confides in me or not.

'Could you tell me where the bathroom is?' I ask. 'I've drunk too much water.'

When I'm safely ensconced in the bathroom, I take out a prepaid mobile from my pocket and dial her house phone, praying there won't be any interference.

I change my voice to Sam's and make myself sound drunk.

'Hello?'

'Inez, sweetie, how's tricks?' I slur.

'S-Sam?'

'That's right. Remember me, darling? I miss our chats.'

'Erm, h-how's the new job?'

'What new job? Ohhh, that's right. Poor Inez. I didn't leave, honey. Ed just told you that so you'd stop being so paranoid.'

'What do you want?' Her tone goes cold.

'Oh, babe, well I'm drunk, and I just wanted to let you know that your husband's cock is a-maz-ing. I almost couldn't fit it in my mouth.'

'W-what?'

'No, I didn't think he'd have told you. That's why I'm calling. I think you deserve to know. There's no conference. We're holed up in a hotel in London just fucking. I've come out to get something to take back for us to eat, instead of each other. Such an appetite. Anyway, I thought you should know, Ed's planning on leaving you.'

There's an anguished squeal.

'He says he likes me best because I have a more responsive pussy.' I laugh and put the phone down.

I hide the phone and flush the toilet. Then I head back downstairs.

I find Inez in a heap on the floor, tears pouring down her face as she presses keys on her phone, no doubt trying to ring her errant husband.

I can hear the reply. *The number you have called is currently unavailable.*

And it is. Because Edward is otherwise engaged – against the wall of my old family home, with his phone locked in a drawer there. Turned off.

Ed always did insist on walking to the gym early every morning. That's the thing with routine. You know where someone is going to be at a certain time of day. So, I knew Ed would walk past the derelict industrial estate ten minutes away from my old home at six-fifteen am. That's where Bobby stuck a handkerchief full of chloroform in his face before we took him to my house. My parent's old home where no one lives close enough to bear witness to a large man being dragged inside. I paid Bobby a handsome sum of money. He may be a mate, but his silence needed to be bought. I sent him back to my apartment once Ed was secured to the wall.

I put a blonde wig on and my contacts in, so I

looked like Sam again, albeit with puffier lips. At this stage I didn't really give a shit what Ed saw.

When he came around it was so cool to see him freak out about his new surroundings.

'Sorry. I forgot you like routine. I don't think you're going to the gym today, Edward, or your conference.'

I expected him to pull on his chains, but he didn't.

'What do you want, Sam?'

'Simple,' I told him. 'I want to destroy your life. Like you did mine.'


I spend the night consoling Inez. Telling her men are bastards and that she could do better. I lie and tell her I'm sure my own husband has had an affair. That I'm always feeling lonely. She soaks up every word and eventually falls asleep on my shoulder.

I ease her off and go and let Bounty out for a piss. I take out a piece of chicken from my bag that I prepared earlier. Fucking dog had kept barking near it, almost giving the game away.

'Here you go, Bounty. You'll love Auntie Selma's chicken. It's marinated,' I tell her.

She barely chews the meat. It's gone in seconds. Chicken a la antifreeze.

She returns to the warm house, as do I. I place

myself back in the position we were in before. After an hour or so Bounty starts to wobble as if she's drunk. Then she shits herself; the smell is so offensive I want to throw up. A small part of me wants to rush the dog to the vets, but a larger part, the winning part, knows it has to be done.

'I'm sorry, Bounty,' I whisper. 'Sarah will take care of you in Heaven.'

Sarah. That's what I called my beautiful lost baby. I lost mine. Now Inez is about to lose hers.

I wake to another scream.

'Bounty. Oh, my God. Bounty.'

Inez is up and cradling her pet in her arms.

'She had a seizure. Something's wrong.'

'Where's the vets? I can run us there if you like?'

'Please.' She sobs. 'Can we get there fast?'

We arrive. Inez is a dishevelled mess with mascara smears down her face. The vet rushes Bounty into surgery, saying they'll call us.

They phone Inez at home hours later to tell her that Bounty died from kidney failure. That it looked like she'd been poisoned, likely by antifreeze. They tell her that it's so easy for it to happen. It's kept in people's garages. It drips from cars and the pets lick it.

'But she never goes out of my sight.' Inez looks at me, her face crumples as she cries again.

I put a look of terror on my face. 'Oh, God. I let her out last night while you slept. She was at the door, I thought she needed a wee. I wasn't going to tell you because you had enough on your mind, but she ran down the road, and it took me an hour to get her back. She must have done it then. I'm so sorry.' I begin to cry, easily done as I am truly sorry about what I had to do. I had a heart before they broke it. Sometimes it tries to beat again.

'Selma. No. It was an accident. You weren't to know.'

We sit, arms tight around each other and weep. Consoling each other, before I make my excuses to leave, to return to my 'husband,' when really, I'm returning to hers.

## CHAPTER THIRTEEN

SAM/SELMA/MELISSA
3 September 2014

My artwork is almost complete. Edward has been mute for the last couple of days, offering me no physical or emotional response to my news. Today that changes.

'We thought you'd finally moved on.'

It's the first words he's uttered that I believe are honest.

'Well, now you know.'

'To go to all that effort.' He appraises my body. 'There's no trace of Melissa Simmons.'

'Thank God,' I retort, 'Or my surgeon—'

He interrupts. 'I know you lost your husband and your baby, and I can't know what that must have felt like. The betrayal...'

He's trying to get to me. It won't work.

'That's right, you can't possibly know. That's why we're here, Ed, so you can gain some understanding.' I continue with my inking.

'Inez wanted to move. She couldn't stand you watching us. But I told her she'd done nothing wrong. We weren't going anywhere. If anything, I felt you and Dave should move, away from the bad memories of that place. Instead, you spent years taunting yourselves.'

'We spent years bringing up the children left without their mother because of your actions.'

'My actions? You stifled your husband. He couldn't be himself, having to fit in with your playing house games just like when you were at school together. He'd grown up.'

I swipe the alcohol rub from my desk and pour it over his fresh tattoos. I watch him try to hold back the pain but his face grimaces and he groans.

'You fucked my husband, and you fucked me over. If you hadn't instigated this. If you'd left us alone, there'd still be me, Jarrod, and at least one daughter. There'd still be Sandra, Dave, Becky, and Joanne.

'You're fooling yourself. There'd be no you and Jarrod,' he spits out his name. 'Because it was all a fucking lie.'

I grab my tattoo machine and swing it at Ed's head. A huge gash appears on his cheek as his head collides with the wall. He's knocked unconscious.

I check my machine, ensuring it still works and carry on with the final inking while he's quiet. Tomorrow I hope to let him go home - if he still has one.

## 4 September 2014

I walk into the room with a brilliant smile on my face.

'Ed. Darling. Today's the day. I'm letting you go.' I smile, noting the gash to his cheek. His face is no longer clean shaven. He has dark brown stubble. I bet he'd hate his reflection.

He awards me a cold, calculating look. 'Why? Did you finally realise you've gained nothing from keeping me here?'

'You silly billy. What do you mean? I've gained so many things.'

He looks at his chest. 'You tattooed me. I'll have to wear shirts for life. I'll live.'

'Hmmm. How will you explain them to your wife?'

'I'll tell her I was held hostage by Melissa Simmons. The same story I'll give to the police.'

'If you do that, then there's a bounty on your head, darling. You don't think I haven't covered myself, do you? Speaking of Bounty. It's a shame what happened to your wife's dog.'

He strains at his cuff. 'What have you done? You'd better not have been anywhere near Inez.'

'Oh, I've been near her alright. Very near.'

'You can do what the fuck you want with me, but not with her. Do you hear me? She'll have been frantic while I've been missing. She'll have called the police.'

'I think you'll find she doesn't want anything more to do with you, and she doesn't care where you are,' I taunt. 'What with you fucking Sam from work, which is where she thinks you are now.'

'How the fuck have you managed to see her? She'd recognise you.'

I shake my head and remove my wig to show him my cherry red hair. 'Nah. She's looking for a blonde she saw once in a photo. Not her best friend Selma.'

'Selma? You're fucking deranged.'

'I certainly am. Congratulations. You made me this way.'

'I don't know how you keep up with your multiple personalities.'

'It's all an act. I think I'm actually really fucking clever and that's what you didn't bargain for when you fucked over a meek little housewife.'

'Do it then, let me out. I won't go to the police. I'll sign something. Bring me a fucking legal document. I bet you have one.'

'Of course I do. Legal documents and your demise plotted should anything go wrong. Yours and Inez's. I'm not choosy over whichever one of you rots in hell.'

'All I want is my wife. All I ever wanted was my wife.' Ed's face shows actual pain as a tear runs down his cheek.

'Except to get your wife you had to steal my husband, didn't you?' I spit. 'So, I didn't just lose my baby. You fucked up my husband so badly he relinquished his whole self and became Inez Bonham. You screwed up my world.'

'He was never yours.'

'He was always mine,' I spit. 'Then he ceased to exist. Have you any idea what that was like? I almost died. I had to have counselling. I'd lost my baby and my husband. I find out when I'm conscious that my husband wears dresses; a long dark wig, that looks like my own fucking hair, and you've named him Inez. He didn't even choose his own fucking name. He looked a complete joke. You made *me* a joke. I had *nothing*,' I scream.

'I did what I had to do,' Ed says quietly. 'He was mine more than he ever was yours.'

'You. Stole. My. Life,' I spit out. 'Now you've lost her. Good luck with getting her back.'

'You stole mine first, you bitch,' Ed snaps. Then he looks shocked.

'What do you mean?'

He tightens his lips. His jaw tense. I can see he's not going to tell me anything.

'Oh, Ed. Just when I'm ready to let you go, you show me you have more to tell. I'm intrigued.' I drag my nails up his arm and hold his chin in my hand. 'You're not leaving today after all.'

I leave him in the room. My phone rings. Inez wants to go out to the pub. It's eleven-thirty am. She's having a bad day. I grab my things. I'm sure I'll be able to turn this to my advantage.

# PART 2

## INEZ

## CHAPTER FOURTEEN

Inez

I was born Jarrod Lee Simmons.

I remember finding it hard to make male friends at school. I didn't want to play football. I wanted to play with the girls and their dolls. I wouldn't let my mother cut my hair short, preferring it to my shoulder and wavy. Luckily mullet hairstyles were all the rage back then and my hair hadn't thinned like it did in my mid-twenties. Mel was my best friend from us being five years old. We met in the first year of infants and were inseparable. She had been fed fairy stories from birth and decided I was her Prince Charming. We even got married in class. She looked so pretty in her dress-up wedding dress. I kept playing with the net of it.

I kept my dirty secret to myself. In my teens, I couldn't understand why I'd want to wank to pictures of both men and women and yet hate my penis and wish it didn't exist. I'd steal clothes from Mel's house. She had so many she never even noticed. Every so often her mother would make her clear out her unworn clothes and put them out on the street in a bin bag for the charity collection. I'd come back later that night under cover of darkness and go through the bag, taking out the items I liked. When we were thirteen, Mel was actually taller than I was by a few inches, so the clothes lasted me a long time. When my own height shot up to six feet, while she stayed five foot five, I couldn't raid her clothes anymore. I'd pretend to buy makeup for my mother, saying it was her birthday. At night, I'd lock my door and put on makeup and a skirt or dress, and I'd sit in my room feeling normal.

The first time I realised that my sexuality was not defined by the sex of a person was when I went on a camping trip with the Scouts. I'd met a young guy from a different group a couple of times. I confessed to him about my feelings, and he understood. He kissed me, and we fooled around. I met up with him a few times afterwards, and we progressed to anal sex, but it couldn't last. I had to end it.

Mel and I became lovers when we were fifteen. I guess I'd resigned myself to the fact that my life would be spent with her. To be honest, I was fascinated by her soft breasts and her warm pussy lips. I tried to imagine I had them. I'd quiz her all the time on how it felt when I touched her. She thought I was an attentive lover, but actually, I was a jealous one. I didn't much care for sex. It was too confusing for me with my male genitalia and female mind. I'd get off and then feel guilty about it. Sometimes I'd imagine that scout boy was sucking me off. Other times I'd get Mel to sit on top of me, and I'd try and visualise that she was fucking me. That the penis was hers.

When Mel encouraged me to attend the street poker evening, she had no idea what a can of worms she'd opened. When Edward opened the door, my jaw dropped to the floor. He'd really not changed that much from the young scout who's dick I'd fondled. He confessed to having kept tabs on me, asking people we knew where I was and what I was doing. He told me he'd stood outside the church on my wedding day and wept. He said I'd been the only person to have ever given him love. I was confused at first. We'd been teenage boys experimenting, that's all, but then the other men on the estate had gone home and left Edward and me alone.

He'd held my face in his hand tenderly, leaned over and kissed me.

After having only ever kissed Mel other than Ed, he took my breath away. His mouth was firm on mine. Not the softness of Mel's but hard, commanding. Hunger opened within me that I'd never experienced before. Want. Need.

Edward had taken me to his bedroom, laid me down against his sheets and moved over me. We'd kissed hard for hours. His hands had roamed my body and mine his. He took my rock-hard cock into his mouth and sucked me off. I'd loved it, and I loved it even more when he lubed my anus and his cock, and he took me there. He faced me as he did it and it was like I'd made love, finally, like a woman. I knew then that I needed Edward. But I owed Mel. She'd been my constant all my life, and I couldn't imagine life without her. Edward needed to be my dirty little secret – for now.

I told Mel we could try for a baby. I'd put the idea off as I didn't want a child brought into a world where their father didn't know who the hell he was. But I felt I owed her. The guilt consumed me. I wanted my cock serviced by Edward, but I'd fuck Mel with it, pretending it was Ed's mouth. She was overjoyed when she found out she was pregnant. I couldn't imagine being a father, and I resigned myself to the fact that I'd handle it when it arose. Mel understood when I said I didn't want to make love to her for the health of our unborn child. Of course, it was a complete fiction. I had no more interest in shagging Mel. I was obsessed with Edward, with whom I was exploring the part of myself I'd not fully understood for years.

People expect transgender people to have a particular sexual orientation. Oh, he's now a woman. So he should like being fucked. It's so narrow-minded. Just like anyone else's sexuality, I find I'm attracted to a person, rather than what they have. I identify as a woman, and when I finally had my reassignment surgery, I physically became the person that I'd always identified with. Edward and I were able to make love as a man and woman, though Edward would still take me anally. For him, I was a person he'd fallen in love with, regardless of my sexual gender.

Edward was a complex man. How complex I didn't realise until we became a couple. After Mel's accident, my grief was crippling. I felt responsible for the death of an infant Mel had wanted from being small. She'd discovered my secret and had lost everything that night, and very nearly her own life.

She was in hospital for months. I waited for her family to visit and tell me what a disgusting individual I was. A pervert.

But Mel came back, and the only thing she wanted was the house. She didn't want me. She negotiated through solicitors, and we divorced. She'd ignore me in the street. I wanted to move, but Edward said we were going nowhere. This was our home, and once Ed made his mind up about something there was no reasoning with him. The truth was that our quiet crescent became a place of safety for me. The game nights and neighbourly drinks had ceased. Everyone kept to themselves, and I was left to become Inez. I'm not sure why Ed chose that name for me. He just said he liked it. I'd always thought I'd choose my own name and imagined being called Lynne, but Ed didn't like that. It was easier to please him. I was happy when Mel married Dave and became a mother to his children. I'd taken away the chance for her to become a biological mother and she excelled at looking after those two girls. I'd watch her from the window when she wasn't looking.

If she saw me and Edward in the street, she looked through us. It was hard having known her for all those years. Her knowing everything about me except for my sexual identity and in some ways, not really knowing me at all. But we'd shared the best parts of our lives together and her not being in mine was a strange loss, a bereavement almost. Edward wouldn't listen when I tried to talk to him about it. When I'd seen the counsellor prior to my surgery, I'd been able to explore it a little. So many opposing feelings in my mind, it was enough to drive me crazy. So, I stayed within my well-ordered life with Edward. Finally able to be the woman I'd always wanted to be, with my regimented but steady husband.

But then he'd got a new assistant. At first, nothing changed, but then she started taking his phone calls. Alarm bells sounded. Edward never relinquished control to anyone. The only times he gave himself over was inside my hand, mouth, pussy or arsehole at the time of release. Suddenly Sam was answering his phone and Edward was unavailable.

He became angry with my suspicion and paranoia, our once ordered household becoming a place of argument. But Edward had never shown interest in anyone but me. When the photo arrived in the post showing a slim, blonde woman I'd lost it and thrown crockery and glassware. She was so womanly. A woman who looked stunning and too good to be real. Bright blue eyes. Beautiful bone structure. A perfectly honed gym body. Glowing tanned skin. Impressive tits. She was the total opposite of me with my brown curly wig and six-foot frame. My hair looked pathetically thin and wispy when I'd tried to grow it, so I'd had to cope with the heat and itchiness of wigs to become the Inez of Ed's dreams. Hormones had given me A-cup breasts and thickened my waist, but exercise would have made me feel more masculine, so my body was soft, my thighs wobbly. Sam was in her twenties, myself approaching fifty. I imagined Edward was having a mid-life crisis, though he was only two years older than me. He was going to take Sam as his younger lover, and I would be alone. The freak show. All by myself.

He was angry. Told me I was being stupid. That there was no one else for him but me. He said she'd left and that he wouldn't be seeing her again. For my sake, he'd let her go.

I believed him. Until the phone call. Now my whole world has fallen apart, and I didn't know what to do next.

I thanked my lucky stars that God brought Selma into my life. I am no longer alone. I have a friend I can seek advice from. Thank goodness she's here.

## CHAPTER FIFTEEN

Selma
1 September 2014

After I left Edward last night, I spent the evening at my apartment. It was lovely to work through a yoga video. To stretch out all my muscles. Then I relaxed and watched a DVD. I sent a text to Inez, checking in and telling her I'd be around in the morning.

So here I am now. She's getting me a glass of water. There are photos of Bounty strewn across the sofa, but not one photo of her and Ed. That strikes me as strange.

She walks back in and hands me my drink.

I make my voice sound soothing. 'So, a stupid question I know, but how have you been?'

She sniffles. It's most unsightly and most definitely Jarrod. He never could be arsed to fetch a tissue.

'Ed won't answer my calls. I'd feel better if I could see him or speak to him but his phone goes to voicemail, and that bitch won't tell me where they are.'

'He can't stay away forever. He'll need his belongings at some point.'

Her face falls as if the thought of him leaving her has only just come to mind.

She turns to me, her mouth quivering. 'I don't know what to do.'

I lightly touch her shoulder. 'Well, do you want to fight for him or kick him out?'

She looks down and swallows. 'I honestly don't know.'

I stroke her arm. 'There's nothing to say you have to decide right now. Just get on with your normal day as best you can and make decisions when they need to be made.'

Inez chews on a fingernail then she stops herself and pulls at an imaginary thread on her top. 'Can I talk to you? Properly talk to you? There's something I want to check out.' Her voice comes out shaky.

'Of course,' I say, moving closer. What is she about to divulge?

'I-I'll understand if this drives you away and you never want to see me again, but well, I-I'm transgender.' She lets out a deep shaking breath. 'I was born male, although I've mainly identified with being female.'

*Fucking what? Mainly identified? Liar.*

I attempt to stay outwardly calm. *Breathe, Mel, breathe.*

'Really? It did cross my mind,' I tell her. 'You're so tall, and I can tell you wear a wig, but I didn't know for definite. It's not highly obvious like you see with some trans.'

Inez sits back, a frown on her face. 'But you seem so accepting of it. Doesn't it bother you? I thought you'd have left by now.'

I look at her as if she's stupid, which she is, but not for this reason. 'Absolutely not. I think my generation are a lot more accepting. I've slept with women as well as my husband,' I lie. 'It's about falling in love with a person not what gender they've been officially assigned.'

'Oh, my God, that's exactly how I feel. I really do believe fate sent you my way, Selma.'

*God, I want to suffocate her with a cushion.*

'So, you say you've always identified with being female? That must have been hard growing up.'

She sits back on the sofa. 'It was. I had no one to confide in. Things were different back then. I didn't believe anyone would understand. They'd have called me a freak.'

'Didn't you have a best friend? Oh, guys don't really do that, do they?'

Inez gazes into the distance before returning her eyes to mine. 'I had an amazing friend who later became my wife.'

'You were married to a woman?' I act shocked.

'For a short while.' She takes a sip of her tea. 'She was my best friend through school. Always had my back.'

'So, why didn't you tell her?'

I'm desperate to know the answer to this question. Why she made my early life a joke and a waste of time.

She slides her finger around the top of her cup as she speaks. 'She loved me, and I loved her. Mel spoke about getting married from the moment we met at age five, and she seemed my soul mate. She just got me, well the me I showed. I was born male, I expected to have to stay male. People didn't suspect my gender identity issues because I was always with Mel.'

'But didn't she guess? Sorry to get personal but what about sex?'

'That's one of the things people don't understand about being transgender if you don't mind me saying. I physically and mentally identify with being female, but I enjoyed sex with Mel when I had a penis. At least, I thought it was okay. It's just that, well, we'd been together and never known anything else. When I met Edward, it was all consuming. I fell head over heels. When I'd lived with him for a few years and had my reassignment surgery, my life became complete.'

I want to be sick. The confirmation that he no longer has his manhood. I know he'd alluded to it, but it shocks me that it's no longer there. The parts that made our baby: his cock and balls, and my womb, gone forever, just like our daughter.

'Wow, I can't imagine. So, how do you get to enjoy sex?' I put my hands over my mouth. 'Sorry, that's so rude of me. I'm so intrigued by the whole thing. You're amazing you know. So brave.'

Inez smiles. 'I've never felt brave. I've always felt a coward. I used Mel to hide my true self, and in some ways, I've hidden while I've been with Ed.'

'Well, maybe while Ed sorts out what he's doing, you should take some time to think about what you want?'

'Yeah.' She nods her head. 'Absolutely. I should. Anyway, would you like me to explain about the surgery? That's if you're interested. I hope you're not squeamish.'

'Would you? I'm intrigued. I may pull faces a little, but I'll try to behave.' I laugh.

'Okay, so I had hormone therapy, something which continues to this day. It helped me grow my breasts and made me more *womanly*, though like you say, at six feet tall, that's not something easily achieved. I had extensive counselling prior to my surgery. Ed supported me every step of the way.'

'That's good.'

'So, in the surgery, they slice the penis and remove the internal penile tissue.'

'Ew,' I say, grimacing, and this time my reactions aren't false.

'They removed my testicles, although they used the scrotal tissue to make my vaginal lips. They turned the penile skin inside out and stitched it back up. It's so clever, there's a piece of erectile tissue that they push through the slit, and that makes the clitoris. They constructed a urinary opening and used my abdominal muscles to make my vagina contract. I was in bed for a week and had to have a catheter. The pain was excruciating.' She looks at me and sighs. 'I'll not go into it any further because I can see it's a lot to take in.'

I grab her hand and squeeze it, then let go. 'Sorry, I have so many questions. You have the parts, but I guess you can't come, right?'

'No, I absolutely can. The stub of penile tissue they use as a clit is fully functioning. Ed and I made love after about eight weeks, and I was able to climax. That's when I realised that although I'd enjoyed sex with Mel...with Ed, and my being in the body I'd always identified with, well, it was mind-blowing.'

Part of me wants to smash his cunt up with a baseball bat, but another part of me is strangely inquisitive, especially when he's admitting how he felt when he was with me. I won't allow myself to think about all this right now. I'll block it until I get back to my apartment. I'm here to fact find. That's my aim.

'So how did Mel take the news of your surgery?'

Inez casts her face downward. 'She never knew. We divorced after she caught me with Ed. She never spoke to me again. Her parents said I was dead to her. I was never able to tell her how sorry I was.' She looks up. 'Is it okay if we change the subject now? I feel exhausted. I will talk about it more another time.'

'Of course. I'm sorry, things did get heavy there, didn't they?' I squeeze her arm. 'Thank you for confiding in me though. I'll have to do the same sometime. I have skeletons in my own closet.'

'Well that's what friends are for.' says Inez. 'Hey, do you fancy going to a cafe or restaurant for lunch? Not Coco's because they'll ask me where Bounty is. Anyway, it's time for a fresh start. It's time for Inez to treat her friend Selma to lunch. I'm not going to sit around waiting for Edward.'

'Good for you. Sounds great.'

'We could do a spot of shopping afterwards. I'd love it if you could come with me to find a new wig. Ed chose this one. I'd like to pick one for myself. One that's not so obvious.'

'You dress nicely. Do you choose your clothes yourself?'

'No, that's Edward too. He advised I dressed classy. The only clothes I had before were the ones I'd stolen from Mel. She was a shopaholic and didn't realise I'd taken things.'

I splutter out my water and quickly make it look like I'm giggling.

'Oh, my God, you nicked your wife's clothes?'

'Yes, and she was considerably shorter than me, so you can imagine what I looked like. Also, she was very girly in how she dressed. I looked rather drag queen until Ed took me in hand.'

. . .

I suffer through an afternoon with Inez. I encourage anything anti-Edward, and she uses her credit card to purchase new outfits and two new wigs. She says its revenge against the cheating bastard. Then she bursts into tears.

I spend time consoling her, giving her a hug, which is weird when she's so much taller than I am. Then I send her home and return to my apartment. Inez needs to atone for her actions, and I need a goddamn shower, I feel like my skin is crawling.

A phone call to Bobby and he arranges for a 'driver' in a suit to turn up at Inez's house on Ed's behalf. The driver tells Inez he's there to collect some of Ed's belongings and that Ed will be in touch soon about collecting the rest. When she asks for identification, he shows her the door key and alarm code. The key I'd taken an imprint of when I first went to her house, and the code she never hid when she opened the door with me behind her. Devastated at being told Ed doesn't plan to stay with her, she lets my driver in to collect some belongings. I make sure he takes all of Edwards clothes. As she stole mine, I'm taking his. An eye for an eye and all that.

When the driver brings them to me boxed, I put

them in the back of my car. The next day I visit a charity shop and hand the whole lot over. The owner checks the labels, all designer. 'Are you sure? You could take these to the dress agency down the road and make a decent amount of money from them.'

'No.' I hold my hand up. 'That won't be necessary. We'd like you to make as much money as possible for your charity. It means a lot to us.'

'If you don't mind me asking, why so many clothes? You've not suffered a recent bereavement have you, sweetie?'

'No. My husband has lost weight, and these don't fit anymore. Any excuse for him to go shopping. He's worse than any woman.' I laugh. It's true. Chained to a wall and only given minimum amounts of food, Ed has already begun to lose muscle tone. I love the fact that he can't get to his beloved gym every morning. The break in routine must be infuriating him.

'Well, bless you. Thank you so much for thinking of us,' she says. I nod and walk out.

As I walk away, I allow myself a last look at the shop's frontage – Angels – a charity set up to help the parents of bereaved children. Maybe the funds raised by the donation can prevent someone turning into me.

## CHAPTER SIXTEEN

Inez
4 September 2014

After spending the first couple of days inconsolable, my mood shifts to anger. It would seem I'm going through something akin to a bereavement. When Ed had his clothes collected it was a wake-up call that he really had moved on. Perhaps he needed to fuck another woman, get it out of his system and then come back? Maybe he needed a proper vagina now, a regular life? Who the fuck knew, seeing as he wouldn't speak to me. I had hours alone, to think things through. I realised that I'd spent my life playing a fiddle to someone else's music. Who was I? Who did I want to be? I was neither Jarrod, son of a fervent Christian father who would have turned in his grave if he had seen who I'd become, nor did I want to be Inez anymore - manufactured by Ed and a group of physicians. I wanted to be me.

I need to get out of this fucking house. Its greys make me gloomy, and the empty pet basket hurts my stomach. I need to let rip somehow. I pick up my phone and press my hotkey to Selma.

'Fancy a drink somewhere?'

'It's only eleven-thirty!' she mocks.

'It'll be after lunch by the time you're ready. I need to get drunk. Life's a bastard, and I need a rest from it.'

'Where and when?'

Fantastic. She's such a support. I don't know what I would do without her.

The first thing I do is order a beer. I stick to a half. Ed always poured wine and said beer was unladylike. He'd let me drink beer at his house when I was Jarrod, but once Inez existed, it was wine only, or a glass of champagne – which was like piss. I guzzle my beer down and order another. I can do what the fuck I like today.

Selma strolls into the pub as I'm finishing my second drink and grins. She looks amazing in a long maxi dress with a shrug style cardigan. I wish I had her sense of style.

'Goodness me. Can't even wait?' She nods at my glass. 'What're you drinking?' Then she heads to the bar. She returns with two more half pints of beer. 'I quite like a beer myself. Much better than a glass of wine.'

'Isn't it just?' I smile. 'Selma. I've made a decision. Even if Ed returns. I'm going to be me. Not Jarrod, not Inez. Just... me.'

She looks at me over the top of her half pint glass. 'And who are you?'

'I don't know yet.'

We fall about laughing.

'Well, for now, I think we should stick to the name Inez until you've had a chance to think about a new one. You don't want to keep changing it because you've thought of a better one.'

'I guess I can hold onto that name a little longer. I'm changing though Selma. It's like with Mel I was a caterpillar, camouflaged by leaves. Then with Ed, I've been in a chrysalis. Now I can finally be me. If he doesn't like it, he knows what he can do.'

'While I like your confidence, Inez, I do feel you're

probably having a reaction to your present situation. You might feel different in a few days, or when Ed deigns to get in touch.'

My shoulders fall. 'Do you think so?'

She shrugs. 'Probably.' She puts a hand over mine on the table. 'That's not to say you won't do all those things, but you can't decide your future life in five seconds flat. You've been with Mel and then Ed. Are you going to manage on your own? Will you stay on the estate? Is it your house or Ed's?'

I sit back and sigh. 'It's Ed's house. I have nothing in savings. I gave our house over to Mel through guilt, and Ed wouldn't let me work.'

'Did you use to work?'

'I was an electrician. Not much call for a transgender sparky.' I wink.

'Well if you continue to have those negative thoughts you'll certainly never get anywhere. Anyway, if you're having a new start, you can have a new career. What would you like to do?'

I ponder for a minute. 'Actually, I love makeup. I'd like to work on a makeup counter and help people make the best of themselves.'

'Well, I'm sure you could get a job like that no problem. Why not start looking through the employment websites? Beats sitting at home pining for your pooch and waiting for Ed to call.'

I realise I've drunk another half pint. 'Want another?' I ask Selma.

'I've only had the top out of this one,' she says. 'Would you get me some water? I've got a bit of a headache.'

'Lightweight,' I tease.

'Lush,' She teases back.

The lunchtime rush has come in, and it takes a while for me to get back to Selma. When I return, she's just finishing her half. 'Took you long enough,' I say.

'It's nice to see you like this,' Selma replies. 'It's like a weight's been lifted off you. I'm surprised. After what's happened to you, I thought you'd be in a heap.'

I nod. 'I thought I would be too, but without Edward here, it's showing me what control he had over me. I can please myself now.'

'Oh yeah?' Selma winks.

'Oh, my God, no.' I blush. 'I haven't had any thoughts in that direction.'

'You'll have to excuse me. I need to pee,' she says. 'I don't know how you've not had to go yet.'

'I'm not a lightweight.' I laugh.

. . .

While I wait for Selma to return, one of the bar staff heads over to our table. It's not the one who served me but an older bloke. He looks mid-forties. 'Excuse me,' he says, his arms folded across his chest. 'I've had a complaint about you.'

My forehead creases. 'Sorry?' I look around. He can't mean me, I've not done anything.

'About who you are. What you are.' He spits. 'There's no place in here for your sort. I need you to leave.'

My eyes widen. 'But I haven't done anything wrong. All I've done is sit and enjoy a drink with my friend.'

He looks around. 'And where's your friend now?'

'In the bathroom.'

'Well, I'll ask her to meet you outside. Now let's not have any trouble. Pick up your bag and go, and don't come back – you're barred.'

'And you're a bigot!' I yell. Three halves of beer have gone to my head after drinking them in such a short period of time. My anger about Ed gets projected at this man, obviously the manager or landlord. I stand up, my six-foot frame swamping him by at least five inches.

A woman comes up with her boyfriend. She jumps up and pulls my wig off revealing my own patchy medium length hair. It hurts like a bitch as it was gripped in place. 'Look, it's a ladyboy.' she laughs.

'Get out, queer,' yells her boyfriend.

I grab my belongings, whip my wig from the floor and dash out of the pub. I quickly pull my wig back onto my head and dive into an alleyway. I take deep breaths, taking out my mirror and fixing my wig back in place. That's what's more important. People have noticed me though and are staring.

I hear Selma shouting my name and peek out of the alleyway, beckoning her.

'What's going on? I came out of the loo, and the landlord said he'd thrown you out?'

I start to tear up. 'It was horrendous, Selma, I don't know how I ever imagined I could lead a normal life.' I explain what had happened in the pub.

'Hey,' she says. 'No talk like that. Days like this are going to happen. You have to learn to deal with them. Come on.' She grabs my arm. 'We'll go back to yours and grab a six-pack of beer on the way.'

## Selma

It seems so cruel to hit someone when they're down, doesn't it? A little like, for instance, when your wife's lost your baby and instead of visiting her in hospital you remain with your lover and forget she exists. When Inez went to the bar for our drinks, I rang the bar and told them there was a tall woman in the bar who was a trans prostitute picking up tricks for later. She was becoming well known for it, and they should watch out for her. I'd described her jacket. I didn't know if they'd take me seriously, but when I saw the man from the bar heading in our direction, I'd made out I needed the loo. Then in the toilet, I'd seen a young teenage woman, pissed or drugged out of her mind. She'd asked to borrow my lipstick. I told her she could have it if she did me a favour. It's a Kylie Jenner lipstick, and her eyes went wider than Kylie's lips. I told her there was a 'fucking tranny' in the bar. 'Go and have a look. Drinking beer, dressed in a floral blouse and tight grey skirt. Hilarious.' She giggled. Said it would give her and her boyfriend a right laugh. To be honest, Inez had looked elegant in her new wig, but the pisshead wouldn't worry about that.

By the time I came out of the bar, there's no sign of Inez. The drunk girl nudges my arm as I pass her. 'Saw that drag woman. She was getting thrown out. Fucking queer.' Her boyfriend pulls a face, 'Not fucking normal that.'

I don't acknowledge them further and walk out of the bar in search of Inez, where I intend to console her and act like the best friend she ever had. I laugh to myself. Oh, like I was before when I was Melissa. Only this time I'll be the one leaving and destroying everything in *her* path. I find her in an alleyway, wig dishevelled and with a small group of spectators. I barge past them and dash up to her. Ask her if she's okay. I tell her we'll go to her house. A drunk Inez is an out of control Inez. Time to encourage it and see what further destruction I can cause before I visit her husband and see if he's ready to give up his secrets yet.

## Inez

'Oh, my God, I'm completely smashed,' I tell Selma as if she can't tell when I'm swaying and having to hold onto the walls to walk around.

'Me too,' says Selma, who's let herself go and bought herself a bottle of vodka. She lies back on the sofa and sighs. 'You need some fun. What shall we do now?'

'I think we should have a spend of some of Ed's money, don't you?'

She sits up, 'Yes! Fantastic idea. Get his credit cards.'

'Right, let's max out his cards before he decides to cut me off.'

'What?' Selma looks at me and then closes her eyes as if the effort's too much.

'Selma.' I nudge her. 'Come on. Help me choose some new furniture. This manly shit's got to go.'

Selma opens one eye. 'You need to choose. Time for you to make decisions on your own.'

'But what shall I start with?'

She sighs and grabs the laptop, and types in the name of a top store that sells household furniture and delivers next day for a fee. 'Get on with it. Sofa. Chair. Cushions. Curtains. Rug. Bits of ornament shit. I'm going to sleep. When I wake up I expect you to have spent a shitload of Ed's money and then tomorrow morning, we'll need to throw all this furniture out. I know a charity actually, they'll come and fetch it.'

Selma falls asleep, and I sit back and relax, chilled out from the booze. I order heaps of stuff before I crawl onto the other end of the sofa and close my own eyes.

I wake to find the room in total darkness apart from a touch of light from the moon. I clutch my head and make my way over to the clock on the mantle. It's five am. Selma is still asleep on the other side of the sofa. She looks so peaceful. The moon casts its light across a cheekbone. She's so very beautiful. I reach over and gently touch her cheek to see if her skin is as smooth as it appears. It is. The pads of my fingers sweep across her brow. I don't know whether to leave her to sleep here or tell her she can use the spare room.

With my hand still on her face and while I'm lost in thought, I don't realise that Selma has opened her eyes. Her eyes widen.

'Sorry. I was just, well...' I flush red. 'I wanted to see if your skin was as smooth as it looked.'

Selma sits up a little and pushes her hair out of her face. Her grey eyes fix on mine. 'And was it?'

'Yes. Your skin is so soft and beautiful. I wish I could have skin like that.'

She brings her hand up to mine and runs her fingers down my face. 'Inez, you are beautiful. Can you not see that? Both inside and outside. I can see it. Let me show you.'

She leans forward and puts her lips on mine. I hesitate. Selma is my friend, and if I go here, I could lose her. Then I think of Ed and imagine him fucking that Sam bitch. Next, I stop thinking at all.

I move my lips against Selma's. Then press harder against her mouth. Her mouth opens, and her tongue seeks mine. I'm so used to being directed by Ed in what we do that I decide to take charge. To see what it's like to fuck someone how I want to. I stop and ask Selma to come to my bedroom.

I'm sure she's going to say no, leave, and I'll never see her again. Instead, she nods her head and follows me upstairs. She said she'd had both male and female lovers. Now she was about to fuck a mixture of both. I go with my gut feelings and my longings and don't question whether I'm playing a male or female role. I just have a need, an urge, to make love as myself. Not as a cuckolded husband and not as a controlled wife. I strip Selma of her clothes and find myself in awe of her body. She's toned, with definition to her arms. Her breasts are medium and pert, they could almost be false, but I guess it's the exercise that made them this way. She pulls my top over my head and unfastens my bra. I fold my arms across my chest.

'No. Don't hide yourself,' says Selma.

I remember my promise to own this and drop my arms. I lift Selma and place her on the bed, then lie at the side of her propped up on pillows.

'Let me look at you,' she says.

I lie back. Selma's gaze on my body is so intense I imagine I feel a burn. She strokes my cheek, a flash of longing on her face. Her fingertips trail down my neck, scratching there. I turn my neck and push up into her fingers, the feel of her nails on my skin is divine and causes goosebumps. Further down, she trails her fingers across my chest and then cups one of my breasts in her hand. She palms it, my nipple hardening under her touch. She moves to sit astride my legs so she can gain a better reach and takes my nipple into her mouth. Her hands still roam my body, gently scraping my skin with her nails. I'm on fire. I love being scratched. There's a connection between us as if she knows how to touch me. I'm lost. The alcohol and sensations have me in their thrall. She moves off me and reaches for the zip on my skirt.

I grab her hand. 'Not yet,' I say, and I flip her over.

I sit astride Selma's body as she did mine and trail my tongue down her neck, dipping into her ear. I feel her shiver beneath me. I move lower, trailing my tongue over her toned stomach. Parting her legs, I pause, staring at her pussy. Unlike mine, hers is damn perfect. Natural. I place a finger on her and rub the wetness there. Fascinated I suck on my finger tasting her juices. I never went down on Mel. Could never look at her pussy. I was too confused over how I felt about my sexuality and too damn jealous that she had one and I didn't. My head lowers to her pussy, and I lick there. She bucks against my mouth and tongue. I must be doing something right, despite my cunnilingus virginity. Ed has always adored my blowjobs though. Selma pants and comes against my face, then she grabs my head and drags me up her body.

'It's your turn. Tell me what you want me to do?'

I open my bedside drawer and remove a five-inch dildo and some lube.

Selma takes them off me and looks to me for direction.

'My pussy doesn't get wet like yours does. That's why I have the lube.'

'Do you come the same?'

I nod. 'You'll be surprised.'

The hormones I take make my orgasms strong and plentiful. Selma rubs plenty of lube over and into me and over the tip of the dildo. I lie back against the cushions, close my eyes and spread my legs. There's a pause. Selma is still, so I open my eyes to find her drinking me in. I guess it's not often you get to look at a made vagina.

'It's so realistic,' she says.

'Yes.'

'You really are female now?'

'You sound surprised?'

'It's one thing to be told it and another to see it with your own eyes.'

'Do you want to stop?'

'No,' she says. 'But I want you to close your eyes.'

I feel the dildo nudge against my entrance. Selma rubs it around my formed clit. She rubs her fingers around me too. She's clumsy, and at this point, I bite my lip as I really miss my husband. I wonder whether to stop the whole thing when she begins to push the dildo inside me and then there's no turning back. I love the feel of it inside. I feel home. Though it's Selma making the moves, in my mind, Ed is filling me with his dick, fucking me with his precise and controlled movements. He's ordering me that I'm not allowed to come until he says so. Anger burns through me as I imagine his cock in this Sam woman and in my mind I'm defiant. I won't be told when I can come, I'll do it now. I will fuck this other cock until my pussy hurts. My hips rise, and I grind against the dildo. I feel flesh against me and open my eyes to find Selma holding the dildo against her pussy like it's a dick and is fucking me like a dude.

'Close your eyes,' she whispers.

Her thrusts become more powerful. 'Come for me, Inez,' she shouts. 'Fuck me.'

'Oh, my God, Selma, Yes.'

I push myself on the dildo in a frenzy until I explode.

I sigh with the release and lie back against my pillow. Then I wonder what the fuck I've just done and regret hits me like a sledgehammer. Selma excuses herself to use the bathroom, and when she's gone, I weep like a baby.

## CHAPTER SEVENTEEN

Selma

I rush to the bathroom and switch on the shower, taking care to remove my watch and place it on the window ledge. I grab a folded, clean small towel from the shelf and scrub every part of my body until it feels raw. I sit on the floor of the shower cubicle gagging. I'd not considered that Inez might develop feelings for me, but when she'd reached over and put her lips on mine, I had to make the decision to go for it. His lips felt the same as they always had, warm against mine, taking me back to when we'd been Mel and Jarrod, and I thought we'd been happy.

To a time of lies.

I stared at his breasts and his surgically made vagina and could have wept for the fact that Jarrod was absolutely no more. Another reminder that the formative years of my life had been a complete waste of time. I'd lived with a liar in a sham of a relationship. My whole early life a deception. Of course, I knew one fact, one truth, that Jarrod had loved to be tickled and scratched. So, I used that information against him. My dramatic arts skills had come in useful when I'd faked an orgasm. In my mind my legs were wrapped around his head in a stranglehold, crushing his windpipe, laughing as he clutched for air.

Then I had to fuck him with a dildo. The only reason I was so enthused was because the watch on my wrist has a video recorder on it. I made sure to get a decent angle of the dildo thrusting in and out while she ground herself furiously on it.

'Come for me, Inez,' I had shouted. 'Fuck me.'

'Oh, my God, Selma, Yes.'

Feeling calmer, I turn off the shower and dry myself off with a clean bath towel. I feel cleansed of the dirty deeds of the last hour. Now I need to go back to face Inez, try and salvage the friendship because I'm not doing that again.

A smile breaks out on my face as I watch the video clip. I can't wait to visit Ed.

I walk back into the bedroom to find Inez with puffy eyes. She looks at me, a desolate look on her face.

'Can I say something?'

She nods.

'We were intrigued and pissed. Can we forget it happened? I much prefer you as a best mate.'

Inez rubs her eyes and sits up. 'Seriously? That would be okay with you? I'm so sorry. I was thinking about my husband the whole time.'

'I have to confess, it didn't do a lot for me. I prefer my husband too. Let's forget it. I guess it'll be weird for a bit, but I'm willing to try if you are.'

'Yes please.' Inez grabs my hand. 'You're my only friend, I don't want to lose you.'

'So, your furniture is coming this morning.' I remind her, changing the subject. 'Shall we grab some breakfast and get ready for some interior design?'

'I think I'd better not drink so much ever again,' says Inez as she looks around at her newly furnished lounge. It's unrecognisable apart from the previously grey walls and light grey carpet. There's a comfy charcoal sofa and matching tub chair. Lime green curtains, with a matching rug and cushions. New ornaments. A woodland picture on the wall and a large, lime green, floor-standing vase.

'You certainly know how to shop.' I laugh.

The charity I help had been to collect the old furniture. I kept out of the way in case it was someone I'd met before, but it was two strapping blokes, who moved the furniture like it was made of cotton wool.

'I think we need pizza for lunch to celebrate,' announces Inez. 'It'll help the remnants of my hangover too. You fancy some?'

'I'd love some.'

Inez grabs her coat. 'I'll ring it in, but it's quicker to collect. Will you be okay here while I fetch it? I'll be about twenty minutes or so.'

'Absolutely.' I pick up the remote. 'I'll find some trashy TV programme we can watch while we eat.'

Of course, the minute she leaves I explore the house. I find Ed's office and look through his stuff. As I rifle through his drawer, I see a photo similar to the one in his address book. The picture is of Ed in his Scout uniform, but this time he's with another boy – Jarrod.

What the actual fuck?

I leave the room and return to the sofa downstairs. My mind flips out with this new information. They knew each other before? Edward moving to our street had not been the start of my life falling apart? Had he moved here deliberately? Had they been having a relationship all those years or was Edward a stalker? Maybe he'd met Jarrod at Scouts and then started an obsession?

With not being able to confess to having seen the photo, there's only one thing I can do.

I wait for Inez to return to ask how she and Ed met. I wonder if she'll tell me the truth.

Firstly, I make up some shit about my imaginary husband. How his book is coming along. How I miss him when he's in the writing cave because I love him so much. I say we met when I stumbled across an author event when I was on holiday, and he was a signing author.

Then I slip it into conversation. 'How about you? How did you meet Ed? How did you know he was the one?'

Inez sighs and looks at the floor, and for a moment I think she's going to tell me she can't speak about it. Then she looks up.

'I guess seeing as we got a bit too close physically, I may as well let you in mentally. It's not a pretty story, and I'm not proud. Promise me you'll not judge me? I don't want to lose your friendship.'

'I promise,' I tell her.

'Ed moved into this house. I lived down the street with Mel.' She walks over to the window. 'In that house, over there.'

I make a pretence of seeking out my old home.

'Mel encouraged me to attend one of the street's game nights. The guys would play poker and stuff. I hated the thought. I'd rather have been doing the baking she spent her time doing, but she insisted. When I went to Ed's house, and he opened the door, I was shocked. We'd met before, years ago when I was in a scout camp. I'd seen him on a couple of occasions at Scouts, and well, we'd experimented together. The first indication to me that I was not living the life I was meant for.'

'What an amazing coincidence. It was like fate,' I say, faking excitement.

'No.' Inez shakes her head. 'I didn't know, but he'd kept tabs on me. He admitted to having never forgotten me. He said he had to know whether I was genuinely happy with my wife or whether there was a chance for us.' She rubs the back of her neck. 'I started a relationship with Ed.'

## Inez

For a brief moment, I feel Selma is judging me, but the look disappears from her face. 'Did you not love your wife?' she asks.

'I did. It's hard to explain. We were best friends, and I don't remember ever not loving her. Like I said before, sex was okay but nothing amazing.'

Selma winces.

'I know. It's not kind of me to say that, but I was her only lover, and I know now I wasn't a good one. I was always trying to put her off. With Ed, something clicked. I fell *in love* with him.'

'So you left?'

'Not quite. One night we were drunk and got carried away. Anyway, Mel and another guy's wife saw us. Then she had an accident, and well, then there was no more me and Mel.'

Selma looks shocked. 'Oh, my God. What happened? Did she die?'

'Gosh, no. It was terrible though. She was in the road after she found us and a taxi hit her. In time, she remarried. I think in some ways it did her a favour. She seemed genuinely happy with her new husband.'

'How can you know that?' Selma snaps.

I sit back, my mouth open.

'Sorry,' says Selma. 'I'm being judgy. It's just you say she saw you and then ended up in hospital, and you think she was happier afterwards. Did you never talk to her? Explain?'

'No,' I said. 'I've always been a coward. Is that what you want to hear?'

'If it's the truth, yes. We're friends. Talk to me.'

'Fine.' My nostrils flare. 'I was a shit scared coward. She lost our baby, and I didn't want to have to see her. The truth is I hadn't wanted the child anyway. I was sad she'd lost it but happy that I wouldn't be tied to her now I was in love with Edward. Ed didn't want me to see her so I didn't visit and it was easier to avoid all the drama that would have come with it. By the time she came out of hospital all she wanted was the house. She'd grown indifferent to me. So, she got it.'

'Jesus, Inez, what a mess.'

'My whole life was a mess. From then on it was beautiful. Ed adored me. Until now. Until Sam.' I spit the name out. 'Do you know what?' I fold my arms across my chest. 'He's not ignoring me anymore. Tomorrow I'm going to his work, and I'm going to demand he talks to me.'

'Sounds like a plan,' Selma says and smiles.

. . .

Selma

When I leave, I can't put my fury into words. I visit the pub I went to with Inez and hope to God the drunk idiots are still there. It's not really luck. Downbeats like them are never anywhere else. The woman spots me, nods to her bloke, and they saunter in my direction. They try to appear cool, but I can smell their desperation.

'Do you want to earn some money?' I ask them. 'I'll give you half now and half after. You never met me. If you ever grass on me in any way, there'll be an accident with petrol, a match, and your faces? Do you understand?'

I make a deal with them and leave.

Since I decided to keep Ed at my home a while longer, I thought it wise to make him more comfortable. I didn't want him getting sick. Bobby moved him to a bedroom where he could lie down last night, with a bedpan so he could swivel his hips to pee. Of course, for that to happen his bottom half had to be naked, but that couldn't be helped. We very kindly left a shopping channel on so he could spend his day learning about juicers and exercise machines. Tonight I've got him some extra special viewing pleasure.

'Evening, Edward. It's time for this to move along. I want my house back.'

He eyes me coolly. 'That television crap is worse torture than your tattooing.'

I give him a drink, pouring the liquid down his throat and then I feed him a sandwich. The look of loathing he gives me at having to eat at my whim makes a smirk curl the edges of my lips and my heart beat faster with euphoria.

When I'm satisfied he's had enough to eat I ask him my question again.

'What is it you're not telling me, Ed? I know you met Jarrod at scout camp. I know you corrupted him there.'

'He wanted to be corrupted.'

'Whether he did or not, my guess is you encouraged him.'

He smiles and answers my question by doing so.

'Why did I ruin your life? I don't remember you. Was it school? Did I accidentally cause you some kind of problem?'

'Let me go, Mel. This is tiresome, and you're getting nowhere.'

I sigh and sit on the edge of the bed, my shoulders sagging, as if in defeat. 'Were you and Inez always faithful to each other?' I ask him, letting my voice quieten. 'He wasn't faithful to me.'

'Yes. We adore each other. We were meant to be.'

'That's funny,' I say, my voice returning to its usual timbre. I hold up my mobile. 'Because earlier he didn't seem to think of you at all.' I play the video I transferred to my mobile phone.

He watches, his face sears in agony as his wife fucks the living hell out of a dildo that appears attached to my body, hearing her scream, 'Oh, my God, Selma, yes.'

'Guess she doesn't feel the same way,' I tell him.

'You win,' he spits, rattling the chain attached to the bedhead. 'You win, all right. I need to get out of here and get back to my wife. You sick fuck.'

I stand back and glare at him. 'Tell me the secret.' I demand.

'I'm your older brother,' he shouts and then he laughs at me, a self-satisfied smirk on his face. 'Your lovely mother was the school slag, and I was the result.'

'You're a liar,' I scream. 'Permanently creating chaos in other people's lives as if you're the great puppet master. Well, tonight it's time I end this once and for all.'

'Go find out. You're a clever girl. My father's name was Charles Devon.'

I switch the television off and leave Ed in the dark and silence while I dash home to confirm he's a fantasist.

## CHAPTER EIGHTEEN

Inez

The strangest thing happens this evening. I'm on my way to the chip shop, having decided I can't be bothered to cook and I see Dave on his driveway, washing his car. As I'm not with my usual protector, I find my feet crossing the street and stand before him. It's fair to say that he looks shocked to see me in front of him.

'Inez,' he nods, his tone cool.

'Dave.' I say. 'I-' I look around. What the fuck was I thinking? It's talking to Selma about the past that's dragged things up. Made me wonder about what happened with Mel.

'I know it's far too late, but I wanted to say I'm sorry. About everything.'

Dave throws his chamois leather into the bucket of warm soapy water.

'You're quite right, it's too fucking late. Where's your bodyguard, chicken shit?'

I take a step backwards.

Dave shakes his head. 'Oh, my God look at you. I raise my temper and you back off like a girl.'

'I am a woman,' I protest.

'No, you're not. You're a bloke. A bloke I drank beer with. A bloke who had surgery to be a woman. But you're not a woman so don't back off like you're scared of me when you're three inches taller than I am and could take me on any day. Woman or not, you aren't weak, Inez. You managed to turn your back on your family and friends easily enough. Or maybe you were weak and let Ed take complete charge of your life. I wouldn't know because you never spoke to me again. I thought we were friends.'

He turns back to his car, retrieves his chamois from the bucket and carries on cleaning the car's exterior though it's with a renewed vigour.

'Why did she leave?' I say quietly.

He turns around and looks at me like he's sure he's misheard.

'I beg your pardon?'

'Why did she leave? I thought you were happy together?'

'What we were is none of your business, but if you believe she could stay forever in a street housing her ex-husband and his psycho lover, then you're even more stupid than I gave you credit for.'

'Where did she go? To her parents?'

'Her parents are dead, not that it's any business of yours, so no, she didn't go there. You've no right to know what happened in her life and I'm not telling you.'

He picks up the bucket of hot water. He tilts it as if ready to throw it at me. 'Now get off my property.'

'He's left me you know?' I say. 'Fucked off with a secretary from work. Sam they call her. Sam with the perfect vagina.'

Dave puts the bucket down.

I fight back the tears, some of sadness but more of frustration that I'm breaking down in front of a man I've ignored for years. One who I never consoled when he lost his own wife. So I'm surprised when he asks me to come inside.

I settle on his sofa. As I glance around, I see no pictures of Mel, so I guess their separation was acrimonious. There are pictures of youngsters. Dave sees my interest.

'My grandchildren,' he says.

'Gosh. Time passes so quickly.' It's one of those statements you say without thinking, a platitude. I instantly regret it.

'Time hasn't passed quickly for me, Inez. It's mainly been fighting for survival. Keeping going for my children. Waiting for a day when everything resembles normality. When I'm curled up on the sofa with a loved one and all we have to worry about is what we're going to watch on the TV. Instead, I've found myself alone twice, and I blame you and Edward for both.'

'I couldn't help it,' I try to explain. 'We loved each other with an intensity that burned through common sense.'

'Well, it's obviously extinguished now, if he's taken up with this Sam. Is he not coming back then? Is he with her now?'

My voice thickens. 'I think so. He won't talk to me. Hasn't since he left. It's her calling all the time. I'm going to his work tomorrow to demand he speaks to me. I need to know what's happening. I can't stay in this limbo.'

He scratches his chin. 'I thought something was

going on. I saw the charity van come and collect furniture and I've seen you've had a friend round a few times?'

'Selma. She's been my rock.' I tell him. Though I fucked up there as well.

I pour my heart out to this man as he sits in silence listening intently. When I tell him I slept with Selma, he grimaces. 'I know. I fucked up,' I tell him. 'But seriously, it's weird, we've slotted straight back into being friends. It's as if last night didn't happen.'

'So where's Selma now?'

'She's gone back home to her husband. He's a writer apparently.'

Dave shrugs.

I stand up. 'I'm sorry I blurted my problems out. I know it was inappropriate. Thank you for inviting me in and listening.'

As my eyes meet Dave's, I see his are cold and flat. He sneers. 'You always were a cry baby. Moaning that your wife wanted to start a family. I swear Ed must have been a cross dresser because you've always hidden behind his skirts. You never approached your ex-wife or me to see how we were. Then the minute your jailer fucks off, you're over here trying to say sorry. You attempt to satisfy your curiosity about what occurred during the years you've missed, and then you have the audacity to sit in the house of my dead first wife and whine that your husband's gone off with his secretary, that you've fucked your friend and now you're a whole ball of regret,' he spits. 'Your selfishness knows no bounds. Your ego is one of the largest I've come across. You're devoid of personality and empty of empathy. You should have died or been hit by a taxi. You. Not Sandra or Mel.'

I back off. 'I think it's best if I leave.'

Dave picks up a baseball bat from underneath the sofa. 'Take off that wig.'

I clutch at my hair. 'Dave, don't do anything stupid.'

He walks towards me and pulls it off my head. Not again. It brings back memories of the pub attack. Again it pulls, making my eyes water. As I see the menace in his face, I begin to tremble.

'You deserve to suffer for what you've done.'

He swings the bat at my body. The pain is indescribable. He inflicts ten blows in all, including three directly in between my legs. I begin to retch. He drags me by the arm to his integral garage. He pushes me in and looks at my shaking body. 'When it goes dark I'll take you back to your own house. Until then you can fucking stay on the floor like the piece of dirt you are.'

Then he locks the door.

I spend what must be a couple of hours on the cold garage floor with my legs curled up and my arms clutched around me, while I weep and wonder what the fuck is happening in my life.

Eventually, the garage door opens. As the light floods my eyes, I wince. Dave helps me up.

'If anyone asks. You're pissed, and I'm helping you home. Say a word, and you'll be in hospital next time.'

I turn to him. 'I won't say anything. I understand why you did it. I'd probably have done the same.' I gulp as a wave of pain hits. 'I know I'm pathetic, but I loved him so much.'

'Loved?' Dave queries.

I fall silent, and neither of us says another word. I open my front door, and once I close it behind me, I hear Dave's footsteps retreat.

I run a warm bath to try and soothe my aching bones. Livid bruises appear on my body. When my body hits the warm water, pain surges and again I'm brought to tears.

Once I'm out I lie on my bed, thoughts of food long forgotten. I reach for my phone to call Selma. To ask her to come over and help me.

There's no answer. Her phone goes to voicemail. I

leave a message asking her to ring me, my voice desperate.

Then I sit back, realising that once again I'm a coward who's asking other people to protect her. It's true. Why do I believe that because I identify as a woman, I'm weak? That that's how I should act. Weak, defenceless and pathetic. Mel never acted that way. She always fought for what she wanted. Except for me, and that's no surprise after what I did to her. God if I could see her again, I'd fall to her feet and beg her forgiveness. I'm so sorry for the pain I caused her when all she ever did was love me. I am a selfish, introspected wimp.

Somehow I fall asleep. No doubt through the shock. When I wake, I get up gingerly and decide that this is the day I take no more shit.

I'm going to work to see Ed. He has some explaining to do.

'He's off sick? That's his excuse, is it? Where's Jack? Can I speak to Jack please?' The receptionist walks away from me. I catch her eye roll in the direction of her colleague. So what if I'm dramatic? I need answers.

Jack strolls through to the reception. 'Inez? My goodness, it's great to finally meet you. How is Ed?'

Jack asks. 'Not like him to be off sick. Must be serious. Anyway, come through to my office. Would you like a drink?'

My gaze darts around the reception. 'Where's Sam? Is she in? I want to speak to her.'

'Sam?' Jack's forehead creases. 'Sam Briers?'

'I can't remember her surname. The woman Ed's been fucking. His secretary?'

Jack gasps. 'Ed's been fucking Sam? Well, I never guessed that.' He looks at me. 'Inez, I'm shocked. He only ever spoke of you. He adored you. So it carried on since she left?'

'Um.' I rub my eyebrow. 'What do you mean left? She's still here. She's been ringing me from the office.'

Jack shakes his head. 'She can't have been. Sam left a couple of weeks ago.'

'You're wrong. She called from here. Told me Ed wasn't at a conference. That he was staying with her.'

Jack sighs. 'Just a minute.' He speaks to the receptionist while I stand with my arms around myself. When he returns his tone changes to that of someone trying to communicate with an infant. 'Inez. Ed's been off sick, and our computer notes say you've been phoning in for him.' He tilts his head and stares at me. 'Are you feeling okay?'

'She's left, and he's not here. He's off sick?' I run

my hands through my hair, then regret it as my scalp is painful. My painkillers are wearing off, and I can feel a sheen of sweat on my forehead. 'D-do you have a forwarding number for Sam? I need to speak to her.'

'I have her mobile number, but I can't give it to you. Confidentiality. How about you sit a moment in the waiting area and I'll go call her, see if she'll speak to you?'

I nod. 'Thank you.'

When he returns, his face is a mask of concern. 'I spoke to Sam, and she's not seen Ed since she stopped working here. She did, however, say that he had confided in her that he was planning on leaving you.' He places a hand on mine. 'I'm sorry, Inez.'

I pull my hand away. Ed's not with Sam? So where the fuck is he, and who's been calling me? I feel myself sweating even more. The pain is becoming intolerable. I feel sick. My thoughts run fast. Has anyone been calling me? Have I gone insane? Have I imagined it all?

I get up from my seat and head toward the door.

'Inez. I'm worried about you. Can I phone anyone to come and get you?'

I stop. Nodding vigorously. 'Yes. Yes please,' I say. 'Here.' I hand him my mobile phone. 'Can you call my friend Selma and see if she'll collect me? I'm not feeling so well.'

'Of course.'

Jack phones and speaks to my friend. He gives her directions.

'She asks if you feel well enough to wait for her downstairs, so she doesn't have to negotiate a parking space.'

'Yes, that's fine,' I tell him.

'I can wait with you if you like?'

I wave him off. 'No, I'm fine. Thank you for the drink. I'm sorry to bring my marriage woes to your door. If Edward calls, will you ask him where he's really staying as it's not with me. I'm going to head for some fresh air now.'

Jack nods. 'Take care of yourself, Inez. At least I realise why Ed's been off so long. Marriage problems are the worst.'

When I reach the foyer of the building, I lean against the stone pillar and breathe in fresh air. When Selma pulls up in her car, I open the door and more or less collapse inside.

'Please take me home,' I ask her. 'I need my bed and some painkillers.'

'What on earth's happened?'

I begin with the events of the previous evening up until the present time. She stays silent but attentive, both to myself and the road ahead. She takes my keys, lets me into the house and helps me upstairs. She runs me another warm bath, and then I climb below my sheets and sleep to block the world out.

## CHAPTER NINETEEN

Selma

Despite my searching on the internet for a Charles Devon I find no information. After a couple of hours, I give up, deciding it's a pile of rubbish Ed's made up to have me running around at his bidding. I had a fantastic upbringing, and my parents were very much in love. Staring at my body, I realise it's been a while since I hit the gym. I decide to go and work out and get rid of some of the tension. It works a treat, and I return to the apartment with a satisfying ache.

. . .

Answering two different mobile phones in my apartment amuses me no end. Jack had no idea he was talking to the same woman twice. Of course, I couldn't go to the office to fetch her as he could have recognised me. Inez was so confused. She was clutching her head in the car and wondering if she was going insane, then clutching her abdomen because Dave had pasted the shit out of her.

Dave.

My Dave.

I've kept away from him. Kept quiet while I've gone about my business. Inez spoke about Sam and Selma. Has he guessed I'm back? That I'm involved?

After Inez had her bath, I passed her two painkillers, except they weren't. They were sleeping tablets. I now have several hours at my disposal. Several hours to spend in Ed's office. I switch on his computer and wait for it to load. Luckily for me, his password for the home computer is the same as it was for work. Once it's loaded, I open his email account and type an email to Bailey's from Ed. Stating that due to personal issues he's handing in his resignation, effective immediately. I use his credit card details to order some cheap, nasty clothes, so he has something to wear later in the week. Then I write to Inez. As Ed's email account is web-based, she'll not be suspicious.

*Inez,*

*I realise I made a mistake. I genuinely believed I was in love with you and we did share some happy years together. But I've realised I needed a proper woman. There have been several over the years. I'm not proud of having cheated. I'm sorry. They meant nothing. It was just sex. However, Sam is different. I love her. So, I won't be coming back. I'll come over sometime tomorrow for the rest of my belongings. I've handed in my notice at work, and I'm going to start afresh somewhere with Sam.*

*I wish you every happiness and hope you can find the same sort of love I have. You'll realise then that what we had together wasn't it.*

That should do it.

At three am, my drunken couple turn up and daub the house with paint. I let them finish before I call the police on them. Stupid fuckers. They try and tell the policeman I paid them to do it. Unfortunately, I'm sober and educated, and they're drunk and stupid, so they're bundled into the back of a police car. A very groggy Inez lies confused on the bed while I deal with everything. I tell her it's okay. I'll get someone to remove the words tomorrow. Not to worry about it. She nods and dozes. I tell her it's time for some more painkillers and this time I do give her painkillers. Very strong ones. Then a short time later I wake her up and do it again, and again. She's so groggy she's no idea how many she's taking. I give her sleeping pills and pain meds.

At nine am, I leave the pill bottles at her side and phone an ambulance, telling them my friend has had a very traumatic night and I've found her overdosed. They arrive, place her in the ambulance and head off at speed. I tell them I'll follow in my car.

Except I won't. Because Selma is not traceable and is no longer needed.

I stand outside the house and look up at the red daubed paint.

*Pervert.*

*Ladyboy.*

*Sicko.*

If she doesn't remember it from early this morning, it should make a nice welcome home present.

I turn towards my car and spot him standing at the edge of the path. He beckons me over.

I walk towards my husband.

He appraises me. Of course, I am nothing like my previous self. He has no idea it's me.

'How on earth can you look so different?' he asks.

My eyes widen. 'How can you know?' I ask him in my own voice.

'You walked towards me with your usual gait. Plus, I've been waiting. I knew you'd do something spectacular, but this? My God. When you stopped contact I knew it was time.'

'So what do you think of the new look?' I ask him and twirl. 'Although this is just one of my many disguises and I'm kind of done with it. I need to get my hair done. I fancy going back to dark.'

Dave smiles. 'It's what's within I fell in love with. Though the outside is hot. Fuck, I've missed you. So damn much.'

'What surprised me the most, Dave, is how much I missed you. I didn't think I was capable of-' I look away for a moment. 'Well, you know.' We stand and stare at each other. 'I'm almost finished. Just a couple more things I need to do and then I'm back. If I can I come back?' My voice trails off.

'The door's open, Mel. When you're ready, come home. Please be ready soon.'

I nod. I don't lean towards him, or touch him because if I do, we're going to end up in bed and I'll never want to leave. I turn and walk back towards my car. I have a busy day ahead.

After a few hours' sleep, my first call is the hairdressers, where I spend four hours having my hair turned to its original brown. Of course, I have streaks of grey now, but we all love the transformational power of a new hair colour, and I'm ready to be as near to the original Melissa as possible. My contacts are gone, and I'm back to speaking in my own voice.

I'm back.

## CHAPTER TWENTY

Inez

I wake up in a hospital bed. A scream tears from my throat and then the pain comes as I realise my throat is sore. A nurse runs in.

'It's okay, love.'

'Why am I here? What time is it?'

She puffs up my pillow, giving me a weak smile. 'Sit back and try to relax. The doctor won't be long. He's doing the ward round and will get here soon. He'll explain what happened. Now, here's some water, take a few sips for me. It'll ease that throat.'

I do what she says. I feel like hell on earth. What

happened to me? As I move I wince and remember my bruising. Then I recall I went to the accountants where I felt confused, then back to mine with Selma. I had a bath, but my memories are vague after that. Did the police come around? I peer up at the nurse, 'I don't remember.'

She pats my arm. 'It's just after ten. They'll be round with the tea trolley soon. A nice warm, soothing tea will do you good. Try not to worry. You're in hospital being looked after, and you're fine. Now, I need to do your blood pressure, okay?'

The nurse checks me over, records details on a chart and tells me someone will be in shortly. I lie back on the bed. Out of seemingly nowhere, a feeling of terror rises and rushes over my body. It's a hot electrical shock type feeling. My skin sweats. I feel clammy, sick, and faint. My heart beats so hard I think I'm going to have a heart attack. I tremble. My breath comes in sharp, fast pants. I struggle in my sheets, trying to get out of bed - gasping for air.

The nurse rushes back in. 'You're hyperventilating. Inez. Breathe. Follow me. Steady. Deep breaths. You're in hospital. You're safe. Come on, breathe slowly. In and out.'

She brings me back to a calmer level of panic, but it's still there, simmering. Waiting to spill over. What the hell happened? Why am I here? I need Selma. Selma will tell me everything I need to know.

'Excuse me?' I ask the nurse once I'm able to speak.

'Yes, love?'

'I need to contact my friend. Is there a phone I can use?'

'If you give me the number I'll ring them for you, love. I don't think you're well enough yet. We can get you set up with the hospital phone system or get someone to bring your things from home. There wasn't any answer from your next of kin.'

'No. He's left me,' I say. My voice quiet.

'Oh.'

She gives me an understanding look as if she's privy to something I'm not. My teeth gnash together. I'm starting to get pissed off with not knowing what's going on.

'I'll be back in a moment.'

A few seconds after she's gone a doctor walks in. 'Good morning, Inez. I'm Dr Walton. Do you know why you're here?'

'No,' I spit out, frustrated. 'So, if you could tell me, that would help.'

'We received a call to say you'd taken an overdose.'

'A what?' I pull at my hair. 'That's ridiculous. I didn't take an overdose.'

The doctor sighs. 'I'm afraid you did. We had to perform a gastric lavage. You'd consumed sleeping pills and painkillers.'

I try and think back. 'My friend gave me a couple of painkillers, but that's all.'

'Your friend told us she'd left the painkillers on the side. She thought you were sleeping but then discovered you were unconscious. There were pills on the bed around you. That's when she phoned the ambulance.'

I sit back. Had I done it and didn't remember?

'What's a gastric lavage?'

'Sorry, medical term. It's a stomach pump. We cleared your body of the drugs. You're going to feel tender for a few days. Now, when we admitted you, we noticed you had bruising to your abdomen. How did that occur?'

'It's nothing. An accident.'

The doctor sighs. 'If you think of anything you need to tell us, Inez, please buzz. Now, because you took an overdose, the on-call psychiatrist will be visiting you this afternoon.'

I narrow my eyes. 'You think I'm mad?'

'We think you need some support. Something has obviously occurred to make you self-harm, and we need to look into that.'

I rub my eye. 'I'm tired. Can I go back to sleep?'

'Of course. Ring the buzzer if you need anything.'

Dr Walton leaves, and I close my eyes. I took tablets? Had my stomach pumped? I need Selma. She'll help me and explain what's going on.

None of this would have happened if Ed hadn't fucking pissed off. Where is he anyway? With this Sam, I guess. They must have been carrying on for months. I bet she's laughing about the fact she convinced me she was still working with him. He's probably taken her away on holiday. I bet he's not ashamed of her. Frustration boils over. I bet that's why he controlled me. Not because he loved me and wanted me to himself but because he was ashamed of me and embarrassed. Didn't want anyone to know I wasn't a real woman. God, I've been stupid.

The nurse from this morning walks back in.

'Have you spoken to Selma? Is she coming in? I need to see her. She'll be able to give me some answers about what on earth went off last night.' I waffle on.

The nurse swallows.

I still.

'I rang the number you gave me, Inez,' she says carefully. 'But it doesn't belong to anyone called Selma.'

I huff. 'Then you must have written it down

wrong. Can I see the number you called, please? I call her on it all the time.'

'It's okay. She explained it all. She's on her way, Inez, and says she'll help you as much as she can. She's been really helpful and told us what stress you've been going through lately.'

'Who are you talking about?'

The nurse sighs.

'I'm going to go and get the doctor back, Inez, for when Mrs Tebbs comes in.'

Mrs Tebbs? I can't have heard right. That's Dave's surname. Mel's surname.

I swallow. 'Who?'

'Melissa Tebbs. Your ex-wife. She explained that you've been suffering with your mental health for a while now. She says she's sorry that she didn't get you help earlier.'

My heart thuds again. I feel the blood drain from my body. Melissa. My ex-wife. Coming here? Answering the phone of Selma. I really am insane. Or this nurse is.

'I don't understand. Why is Melissa answering Selma's phone? What's going on?'

'She explained. Sit back and relax, sweetheart. She says you've been calling her Selma for a while. That you've been hallucinating and imagining she's someone else. She wonders if it's a manifestation of who you wanted to be.' She nods at me. 'She told me about your op.'

The anger takes over. 'I'm not mad!' I scream. 'I've not seen Mel for years. I've been with Selma. She's been helping me since my marriage broke down. My husband. He's left me. Selma helped me. Where is she? Where's Selma.'

Staff rush in and I find myself held down until I agree I'm calm. They keep a nurse by my bed. Apparently, I'm now on one-to-ones because I'm not safe to be left alone.

Maybe I'm not.

# CHAPTER TWENTY-ONE

Melissa

It feels good to be me again. No pussyfooting about, ensuring I speak in the right accent and don't give myself away like I did with Dave. Now I can be me. Or rather, very soon I'll be able to live the rest of my life knowing that my sacrifices of the last few years were worth it, that they suffered what I did and now we're even. Just a couple more things to strike off the to-do list.

The first is to ask Bobby to drop Inez's phone off at the nurse station with a message that I'll be along later.

The second is to deal with Ed.

I unlock the door of my house and walk through, a smile on my face, knowing that the filthy infestation of Ed is on its way out. I open the kitchen drawer and take out the key for the handcuffs and then open the bedroom door. When I walk into the room, Ed is mumbling to himself. His head turns towards me. He looks like a deranged hobo.

'Did you find the truth? Am I finally getting out of here, sis?'

I give him a withering glare. 'You believe that if it helps you. You are getting out of here though, and this is how it's going to go. I'm going to uncuff you, and then you're going to get a shower. Bobby is arriving shortly, and he'll assist you with shaving. We need to get you looking as smart as possible. After that, I'll fix you a drink and a sandwich, get some sustenance in you, and then you can put on this suit. The last nice suit you own by the way as Inez got rid of all your clothes. Bobby will drop you home. You understand it wouldn't be right us being seen together, don't you? Wouldn't want people to talk.'

'And what if the minute you uncuff me, I break your nose instead?' he sneers.

'Well, then you'll not know how to locate your wife, will you? Or is that ex-wife, or even'— I chuckle – 'Late wife.'

He strains on his chain. 'What have you done?'

'It's a little stupid to let you go, without having an insurance policy, isn't it? I've done what I set out to do, we're even-stevens. Now you can go.'

Ed stares at me. His eyes full of hatred. 'I'll do whatever it takes to get out of here.'

Ed is true to his word. He gives Bobby no problems and is dropped off at his door. Unknown to them I've followed in my car and parked down the street. I move nearer to their house, keeping behind foliage and out of sight. I watch as Ed sees the graffiti on the outside of the house. I watch as he picks up a parcel from behind his bin. A whole new set of cheap shit clothes. When he's safely indoors, and Bobby has driven away, I call his house phone.

'Yes,' he says tersely.

'Your wife is on Ward A2 at Southern. At least, she was when I left. They may have transferred her to the psychiatric unit by now. Anyway, I'm about to find out. I'll see you there.'

I cut him off.

## CHAPTER TWENTY-TWO

Inez

They ask me if I'm settled now. I nod. I'm confused still, but I feel a lot better. If Melissa comes, I'll ask her to explain. I don't think I've gone mad. There's an explanation here somewhere, I know there is. I'll bet the drugs they've given me here have made me imagine they've said Mel. It'll be Selma who visits, I'm sure.

Another nurse walks in with my phone. 'This has been dropped off for you.'

I brighten and smile. 'Thank you.' This is great. I can look through my photos and find the ones of me and Selma together. Then I can show them to the nurse. They'll know then I'm not mad. I skim through my photos but find none of us both. I swipe the phone faster. Not a single one. My photos consist of pictures of Ed, and Bounty – my poor beautiful dog.

I check my emails. There are no longer signs banning the use of mobile phones in the hospital, or if there is my nurse stays silent as I carry on searching through mine. I startle as I see that I have an email from Ed. I read it.

*Inez,*

*I realise I made a mistake. I genuinely believed I was in love with you and we did share some happy years together. But I realised I needed a proper woman. There have been several over the years. I'm not proud of having cheated. I'm sorry. They meant nothing. It was just sex. However, Sam is different. I love her. So, I won't be coming back. I'll come over sometime tomorrow for the rest of my belongings. I've handed in my notice at work, and I'm going to start afresh somewhere with Sam.*

*I wish you every happiness and hope you can find the same sort of love I have. You'll realise then that what we had together wasn't it.*

'I need to get home,' I scream. Jumping out of bed

and trying to grab hold of my belongings. 'My husband's coming home to get his things.'

My nurse looks at the door. 'Inez, please get back in bed. You're getting upset again. They'll hold you down.'

I stop and turn to her. 'Read this email.' I hand her the phone. 'He's leaving me. This is the last chance I'll have to see him.'

The nurse looks genuinely remorseful as she gives me a sad smile and touches my arm. 'I'm sorry, Inez. You're neither physically or mentally ready to go home.'

To prove her point, I break down and cry right there in front of her. I've nothing left and can't see the point in carrying on, so they're right to keep me here.

I hear a nurse's voice. 'Look, I'll let you in, but if she becomes upset you'll have to leave. It's been a difficult day for her. Do you understand?'

I try to gaze past the nurse's shoulder to see who's behind her but I can't. The nurse is too tall. I breathe a sigh of relief when Selma's voice comes out. 'I understand, thank you.'

The nurse turns to me and says to press my buzzer if needed. I nod, and then she moves away.

My mouth drops open as behind her stands Selma, but not Selma. Her body is the same, but her eyes are a different colour, and her hair is long and dark. Her hair is like Mel's when she was married to Dave.

'I don't understand, Selma. I'm confused.'

'Hello, Jarrod.' The voice that comes out of her mouth is my ex-wife's. As clear as anything. My hand goes across my mouth. It can't be. I really am insane. It's not possible this is Mel. She's years younger and doesn't look like her. I'm mistaken with the voice. It's Selma. Selma with a new hairstyle.

Selma takes a seat at the side of my bed.

'We don't have long. If you create any fuss, our conversation will be over, and you'll be on your way to the psychiatric unit, so I suggest you shut up and listen,' she tells me. I listen with my eyes shut. It *is* Mel's voice.

I open my eyes and can't stop staring. How can this be Mel? Her skin is not the same. Her cheekbones are not the same. Her nose is different. Her lips are a completely different shape. She's toned and tanned, and Mel was soft, with plump edges and as pale as milk. Mel had no bust, this woman's are, I know, a decent handful. If this is Mel, I fucked Mel. There was no Selma. Never any Selma. It was Mel all along.

'You can't be Mel. I hear your voice, but you can't be.'

'You're not the only one to have reconstructive surgery. It's amazing what money can buy.'

I sit a moment, staring and shaking my head. 'But, why?'

'You killed my baby. I lost who I believed was the love of my life. I lost the ability to have any more babies. You took away my life. It was only fair you lost yours in return.'

'So you set Ed up with Sam?'

She guffaws with laughter. 'I am Sam.'

'What?' I sit up. 'You slept with my husband?'

'No, I most certainly didn't. But that's rich coming from you,' she snarls. 'I'll explain it to you like I did Ed. It's really quite clever when you think about it. It's a puzzle. Rearrange the letters of Melissa, and you get Sam lies. Oh, and how Sam has lied. She lied about having an affair with your husband. I did work with him though, that's the truth. It was so much fun working with Ed and him not knowing who I was.'

If I thought my mind was messed up before it's nothing to how it feels now. I'm reeling. I can't take my eyes away from my ex-wife. Trying to find any part of her I recognise, other than her now non-contact-lensed eyes and her voice. Even the shape of her eyes is different, though other than the colour it's difficult to associate it with the woman I knew.

'So, you weren't ever my friend?' I ask. 'You were playing a part?'

'Yup.' She sits back and smiles. 'Your mugging? Set up.'

I gasp.

'Well, thank you for at least being helpful when I lost Bounty,' I say. I watch as her face saddens. 'I'm still devastated.' I tell her.

'It's the one thing I regret.'

'W-what?' My breath catches in my throat.

She fiddles with the wedding ring I now notice on her left hand. Not the one I put there. 'I made a huge donation to a pet charity after that you know. For them to specifically look into how to develop antidotes to antifreeze poisoning.'

'Y-you killed Bounty?'

She looks at me with an intense stare. 'You killed my baby. I killed yours. Only you can buy another one. How is that fair?'

'So all of this has been for revenge?'

'That's right.'

My forehead creases. 'But all that effort. Surgery to make yourself different, murdering animals. Do you not feel it's slightly over the top? Could you not just have egged the house or something?'

'You still don't get it, do you?' she says. 'You're making jokes about a situation that has no humour.' Her voice is so low, it sends a chill down my spine.

'You tilted my world on its axis. You were my whole life. We were happily married and having a baby. In one night, I lost my husband, who became someone else, so I couldn't even mourn your loss properly. You were no longer Jarrod but still around. Living across the street, shoving your happiness down my throat, making me choke. I fought for my life. I lost my baby and any chance of having one. Then I found out I'd lost my friend. Do you even remember Sandra? She was so guilt ridden she killed herself. Next, I lost my home.' She puts a finger up as she sees me start to protest. 'Yes, I got it from you in payment for the divorce, but it was never my home again. I had to give away all the baby stuff, Jarrod. Do you know how that felt? Of course you don't. You didn't give a shit because you were so in love with Ed.'

I wince as she calls me my old name again, but I guess that's who she's talking to so I let it go. Right now, that's who's present in this hospital room. Jarrod and Mel. Having the conversation we should have had after the accident.

'I'm sorry.'

'No, you're not. You never wanted the baby. That's what you told Selma. Oh, by the way, that's another in-joke. Selma Is. Selma is Melissa. Another jumble of the letters. You'll see I've had to take my laughs where I can find them.'

I bite my lip as I think back to my conversation with Selma. I told her everything. Mel knows everything. Fuck.

'I think what hurt the most though, Jarrod, is that you couldn't have confided in me when we were younger. When you first started things with Ed. Instead, you dragged us through years of lies. Years I could have spent with another man, having another man's children, being happy. Now do you see why you have to pay? Yes, it's taken me years, and I don't care. You already took years of my life so what's a few more? You don't deserve happiness, Jarrod. Not one bit of it. Not with him anyway.'

'I love him.'

'Do you? That's not what I think. I've spent enough time with you the last week to get to know exactly what your relationship was like. He controls every one of your actions. You can't breathe without his permission. You swapped a life of imprisonment with me, for another one. You can be Inez, but you're still not yourself. You're Ed's toy, Inez. He even named you. So who are you?' Her voice rises on the you. 'You're no longer Jarrod. Are you, Inez? Or are you someone else? The person *you* hoped to be. You said you had an idea of a name of your own.' She laughs. 'I was going to say you don't have the balls to do it, to be yourself.' Another laugh, 'and you really don't, do you?'

I look at the bed, concentrate on the hospital emblem imprinted on the bedding.

'I wanted to be physically sick when I saw your vagina.'

I wince and hug my arms around myself, trying to become smaller.

'Not that they haven't done a good job. In some ways it's fascinating, to see how they can make a vagina that actually comes. Science and biology are incredible. But it was like another loss to me, you know. I had to acknowledge that the male part of you was completely gone.'

'I've never felt male, Melissa.'

'I know that now,' she says in a quieter tone. 'You explained it all to Selma.'

'So where's Ed then? Do you know?' I ask her.

'He's been in my old house.'

'The one at Handforth? Your parents old home?'

'Yes.'

'Why has he been staying there?'

'Not through choice. I kidnapped him. He's not the same man either now.' She glares at me. 'We'll see how you get on when he returns. By the way, he knows you fucked me.'

I breathe sharply. 'I'll tell him you lied.'

'I recorded it on a camera on my watch Jarrod. He's seen it.'

I place my head in my hands. 'Oh, my God. What else have you done?'

'Lots of things. An eye for an eye. As I said, I lost my baby, you lost yours.'

'I can't believe you murdered my dog.'

'Then I lost my husband. I can't force Edward not to want you, so instead, I'm sending him back with a reminder of what you stole from me. Let you look at it as you make love and remember. I'll always be there now, Jarrod. Always. In your bedroom with you. While Ed thinks about how you let me fuck you. How you cheated on him. When you look at Ed's body, you're always going to be reminded of me. If you survive it, good luck to you. But my hope is that it eats you alive until you can't stand to be together anymore. You see, I don't want your separation to be quick. I want it to take years. I want it to waste years. For you to realise that it's all been for nothing. Your whole sad fuck-up of a life. All for nothing. That you failed as Jarrod, that you failed as Inez. That you don't know who the fuck you actually are.'

'I never realised how much hurt I caused you, to make you like this.' I look at her in pity.

'Well, now you do,' she sneers. 'Oh, don't give me that look. The poor Mel look that you gave me when I asked you if we could have children and you made me wait. Now I can finally move on with my life. That's if Dave will still have me. I realised how much I loved him when I was away. I couldn't understand it as I'd only ever known the fake love between us. Dave and I - we have to start again, afresh. We're getting on in years now. We don't have any more time to waste. I'm almost done with you.'

'Almost?'

'Like I said. I lost my home. I could never settle in that house. I only wanted it so I could use the funds to pay for this.' She sweeps a hand over her body.

'What have you done to my house?'

'Let's save that for later because any minute now you're going to get a visitor. I can hear him asking where you are.' Mel laughs. 'It's such a shame that I'm going to tell the nurse you're extremely agitated and need a rest before you have any more visitors.'

'Mel. No.'

But she does. I watch her go out and have a word with the nurse outside the door. I hear Ed arguing as the nurse says he can't go in. That I need to rest. That visiting time starts again at six and to come back then. He gets angry, and she warns him that she'll ring security if he doesn't calm down. I hear him storm off, his footsteps heavy and then I hear Mel say, 'I wonder if that's where her bruises came from?'

She's so very fucking clever.

How I underestimated my stay at home housewife.

At six pm Ed bursts through my door. He dashes over to my bedside, his arms wide.

I veer back towards the bed head.

'You can't hug me?' he says.

'I'm not myself at the moment, Ed. I need a bit of space.' I look at him, seeing his drawn face, his weight loss. 'What did she do to you?'

'She tried to break my spirit, but she failed. Other than when she showed me the video.'

I cast my eyes down. 'I'm so sorry.'

'Don't be. If it had been another person, it'd be different. But it was Melissa. She's part of your past, and we'll put her back there again.'

'I want her to be left alone, Ed. She's suffered enough.'

'What?' Ed snarls. 'Are you kidding me?'

'No.' I snap, waving my hand around. 'All this that she did. She explained. It was a reaction to what we put her through. She's finished. It's over now. It's time for us to live our lives and let her live hers.'

He removes his jacket and begins to unbutton his shirt.

'Ed, what are you doing?'

'You need to see this.' He opens his shirt to reveal words. So many, many words. The same word. His abdomen and chest are covered with the words.

MINE.

MINE.

MINE.

MINE.

'It seems your ex-wife wants to remind us that we took from her,' Ed says. 'I'm sorry you'll have to look at these, but at least they'll cover with a shirt. I was scared the stupid bitch might tattoo my head.'

'She's not a stupid bitch,' I tell him.

'Oh, my God, you're seriously not sticking up for her?'

'No. But she's far from stupid. She's smarter than I gave her credit for and now we have to pay.'

'I'll find out the cost of laser removal and see if they can be removed or faded. I might be able to cover them with something else.'

'She told me.' I study his body. 'She said that every time we made love, she'd always be there.'

'What? Because she wrote MINE on my body? Do you know what? We can make this about us. I'm yours. You're mine. We'll work through it.'

I shake my head. 'No. You don't get it. It's part of her word games.'

He sighs. 'You're reading too much into this, Inez.'

'Mine.' I touch the M on his chest.

He clasps my finger. 'Yours,' he says.

'No.' I snatch my hand back. 'Watch.'

I touch the M. 'M is for Melissa.'

I trail my finger across the I and the N. 'IN for Inez.'

I point to the E. 'E for Edward.'

'All three of us.' I trail my hand across the letters and back away from Ed. 'Always there with us.'

'Inez. Don't be stupid. You're letting her get into your head. That's what she wants. Now, what do we need to do to get you discharged?'

'Don't call me that.' Mel was right. I'm not being myself. I'm being who Ed wants. Right now, he wants little Inez to behave and come home like a good girl.

'Look. I've just got away from one nutcase, and I'd really like to go home. Although I note half the furniture has been changed, so it doesn't really feel like my home.'

I flinch at his words. 'Then go. Get away from this nutcase.'

'Inez.'

'I'm not Inez anymore. I always wanted to be called Lynne. That's my name from now on, get used to it.'

He sighs out loud. 'I'm starting to think you really do have psychiatric problems.'

'You're right. I have a lot of problems.' I shake my head in agreement. 'So I'm staying here to work through some of them. They have specialists here. They can help me come to terms with everything that happened and help me to become who I want to be.'

'And what about us?'

'When I finally get discharged, we'll see if you want to be with Lynne, and if I want to be with Edward, won't we?'

'She'll pay for this.' He spits out angrily as he makes his way towards the door.

'Leave her alone. We've caused her enough problems.'

'I'm afraid it's not that simple,' he yells as he storms from the room.

I should feel sadness that he's left after I've only just got him back but I don't. I feel relief. I feel a weight lifted. I smell a fresh start where I can try and make amends for everything that's happened, and I can focus on the rest of my life like Mel is doing.

If Ed will let her.

## CHAPTER TWENTY-THREE

Melissa

It was all set to happen the minute Ed left the house. Bobby had parked up nearby and returned as soon as he saw Ed leave the street in the taxi he'd ordered. Bobby has my key and the alarm code and leaves no sign of forced entry. He's dressed in builder's garb, and so raises no suspicion on our quiet little estate. Anyway, after the scandal that tore us apart, I know everyone would keep their mouths shut if they did see something. They live private lives now. So, Bobby leaves a pan on. It's his last job for me, and after this, he leaves to return to Suffolk. Stupid, stupid Ed. Despite his denial, it will appear he left the pan on and burned down his house. They'll determine due to the stress of a wife in hospital he got distracted and careless.

Dave watches and lets the house become overwhelmed with flames before he phones the fire brigade.

'Thanks, darling. That should do nicely,' I tell him. I walk over to him and place my arms around his neck.

My eyes stare into my husband's, and I try and show him how much I love him with that one look. 'I'm done. They lost what I lost. Now it's time to live my life, our life. Take me to bed, Dave. I need you.'

So while the house down the street is cooled down by the fire brigade, our house heats up.


Dave walks up the stairs, and I follow behind. We enter our bedroom, and I gasp. It's the same as when I left all those years ago, bedding and all.

'I hope you've washed this since I left.' I laugh.

'Yes. It's a little threadbare, but it's you. I wanted to keep everything us.'

I bite my lip. 'I'm sorry.' I sweep a hand down my body. 'I didn't do the same, did I?'

He takes a step towards me. 'You're still you.'

Slowly, he removes my top, pulling it over my arms

and head and letting it drop to the floor. He pours over every detail of my body. He drops the straps of my bra off each shoulder and unclasps it at the back, letting it sweep past my breasts on its way to join my top. His hands explore my new breasts with utter devotion. It's like he's attempting to commit my new body to memory.

'I'm not going anywhere again,' I whisper.

'I can't believe you're here,' he says. The emotion is too much, and a tear trickles from one eye. 'Fuck, I missed you so damn much.'

Hunger flashes in his eyes and he undoes my trouser button, yanking down the zip. My pants follow. He sheds his own clothes with haste and backs me onto the bed, *our* bed, with a frenzy. His lips tease my body, replaced by his tongue. It's at this moment it becomes clear that no matter how different the outside of my body is, it responds to Dave exactly as it did before. Our bodies move harmoniously together, with the assured moves of lovers who know each other intimately. I moan as I accept his cock within me. I need him with a fervour I can't put into words. I indicate it with my body instead, raising my hips off the bed towards him.

'Open your eyes,' Dave says.

We keep our focus on each other as we build

towards our climaxes. Our gaze on each other intensifies. Without restraint we thrash against each other, seeking the point where we reunite in ecstasy.

I feel Dave tighten as I build towards my climax.

I pulse around his cock as he releases his seed inside me.

He lowers his forehead to mine. Beads of sweat cross his brow.

'I love you. Please don't leave me again.'

'I told you, I'm going nowhere.'

He lies back against the pillow. 'I think we should move,' my husband says.

I stroke my fingers down his cheek. God, I've missed him.

'A new beginning. What do you think about moving to the States?'

'I'll go anywhere you want me to. As long as we're together, I don't care.'

I snuggle into his arms and sleep the soundest sleep I've had in a long, long time.

The sleep of a deluded person who believed Edward would let it all lie.

# PART 3

## EDWARD

## CHAPTER TWENTY-FOUR

Edward

I thought my parents loved me. Though my father worked long hours and was gone on many an evening, my mother did her best to bring me up, but she struggled. She overdosed on painkillers when I was twelve. By fifteen I had a stepmother. She ignored me completely until I was sixteen. Then, all of a sudden, as I grew, so did her interest.

When my father returned home after one of his trips away he finds me balls deep in his wife. She'd been quite the teacher, and I had an array of skills that would stand me in good stead in the future.

My father grabbed me by the shoulder and threw me into the door. I'd stood up, ready to escape. But I saw fear on my stepmother's face. Watched as my dad stalked over to her like a cat teasing prey, as he'd taken off his belt and thrashed her until the skin on her back ripped apart, blood trickling down onto the floor. Her screams were beautiful. That's what I remembered, but they couldn't replace the satisfaction I'd got from seeing that fear, knowing that my dad was in charge and would mete out punishment as he saw fit. I got harder from that than I did from thinking about fucking her.

From then on, I ignored her, which my stepmother did not take kindly to. Despite her punishment from my father she continued to pursue me. I'd find her half naked in my room. To her annoyance, I'd walk away. Until one day she said the words that changed everything.

'You're adopted, you know?'

I called her a lying, scheming cunt. Then I hit her as my father had. I took a belt from my drawer and lashed her with it. She was petrified, but she let me do it. Wanted me to fuck her afterwards. So in order to find out exactly what my background was, I fucked my stepmother while her back bled into the sheets.

My real mother was some young slut who'd fucked

another pupil and come unstuck. She didn't want the child because the father was part African American and part Native American. She'd been intrigued enough to get impregnated by him but not enough to stay with him. Did I find all this out on my eighteenth birthday? Fuck, no. My stepmother was the social worker involved in my adoption. Now thirty-eight, she'd been fucking my 'father' since she was twenty-two years old.

So I did what any kid would do. I went to see my real mother. There was no forwarding address for my father. No way of contacting him, but my stepmother, Inez, gave me her address.

Inez.

Are you confused?

Not my wife.

My stepmother. The stepmother I couldn't control. The only person who ever played me. The person who made me the scapegoat, the victim. The name for my future wife was clear, as was her appearance. She was tall like my stepmother. I made sure her hair was dark like hers, and then I gave Jarrod her name. An Inez I could completely control, even to the point where she got herself a vagina. That had been all me. Encouraging Jarrod to be what I wanted him to be - her.

My stepmother had broken me for all women.

None of them ever had that fear. I wasn't a rapist, and when I brought out restraints, they always seemed to enjoy it. I began to despise them. There may be a spark of worry, but they knew their fuck was coming and went along with the ride. Never any fear. Until Jarrod.

When I walked down my mother's street and stood at her fence, I found a dark-haired girl and a fair-haired boy chatting away while the girl hosed the garden plants.

'Hey. Excuse me. Do you know where Hendon Street is?' I asked.

The girl looked at me coolly, as if annoyed that I'd disturbed them. The boy moved away from her and over to the fence. 'Sure, it's down the street, left and then left again.'

'Thanks.' I said and wandered away. I'd taken note of the scout group badge on the shirt he was wearing. I wasn't sure why. I just collected it. Another piece of information. I hung around the house a few times at different hours of the day until one day I got lucky. My real mother was in the house alone; the daughter and her husband, along with the girl's male friend, had got into a car filled with fishing equipment. They were going to be a while, and I had the opportunity while they were out to net my own catch.

I can remember it so clearly. I rang the doorbell, and it was pulled open quickly.

'What did you leave this-? Oh. Can I help you?'

Her request was a hope that her eyes were playing tricks on her. For my colouring, the same as my adopted father's, was also the same as her ex-lover's. She didn't want it to be true, but she knew.

'You have his eyes,' she said.

She invited me in. I kept myself cool, controlled. I would wait to hear what she said before I made decisions about her future and mine. I found out over a cup of tea and a slice of apple pie that she had wanted to keep me. Had fought to do so, but at fifteen, she had lost the battle against her parents and had given me up. She cried as she explained how she'd tried to get over it by marrying at seventeen and having another baby. But that it hadn't worked. For as much as she loved my half-sister Melissa, it had never replaced the hole left by the loss of myself.

My mother had wanted me. It was like she gave me approval. She hadn't abandoned me. She had fought for me. It was my grandparents who were to blame. She was estranged from them, she explained. Would never have anything to do with them again.

So I asked what would happen now we had found

each other again. My mother faced me with a look of stoic regret.

'We go back to how it was, Edward. I have a daughter now and a husband. They don't know about you. If word got out, I'd be a disgrace. You need to return to your life, and I'll return to mine. Just remember, I wanted you.'

Wanted. Past tense.

She went into a drawer in the kitchen and extracted an envelope from deep at the back. I saw her scratch the top of her fingers as she pulled it out. She checked the envelope and passed it to me. 'There are a couple of photographs of me and your father, and there's some money. I saved it for you, for if you ever came here, though I didn't expect you for another two years at least.'

'My stepmother told me.'

'Oh?'

I didn't explain further.

'Could you wait a moment?' She stood on a kitchen chair and reached to the back of a high up cupboard, bringing down a faded blue elephant. 'For the short time I held you in the hospital you had this toy.' I saw her swallow and tears swam at the bottom of her eyelids. 'Your adoptive parents wouldn't take it. Said they wanted a totally fresh start.' She bit her lip.

'You say you have a stepmother? Your parents split up then?'

'My adoptive mother killed herself,' I said bluntly. 'I don't seem to have a good track record with mother figures. The first abandoned me when I was born, the second when I was twelve, and my stepmother likes to fuck me for her own amusement.'

My mother stepped back and clutched a hand to her chest. 'I'm sorry I can't do more, Edward. I have too much to lose.'

I nodded because I understood. It was a choice she needed to make, and I fully got her position. To keep the life she had intact, she couldn't open the door to the past. No. I didn't blame my mother at all.

I blamed Melissa. Because if she hadn't existed, my mother would have let me in. Instead, I was a dirty little secret. Sent secret parcels at birthdays and Christmas.

I forced myself to date girls from Melissa's class, without her ever seeing me with them. I found out everything I could about her. She was the perfect student. She was on all the school sports teams. She'd been Head Girl at school. She had the most amazing boyfriend, Jarrod, and they already knew they'd get married and live happily ever after. I'd go home and hit my stepmother, unleashing my anger. Then frustrated with my own weakness, I'd steal from my father's wallet. He always carried far too much money. He didn't know what the hell planet he was on half the time he was so busy with work and my stepmum. It wasn't a lot of money, but it was a start. Myself, I was strong in one subject only - mathematics. So I gave it everything I had. Though I spent my seventeenth year calculating a lot more than sums.

I joined a scout group and became an explorer. I genuinely loved it and wished I'd joined when I was younger. The rules appealed. I felt pride every time I earned a badge. They taught skills - camper, chef, leadership. They made me feel like an expert. We had to abide by the Scout Law, agreeing that we could be trusted, loyal, friendly and considerate, that we'd have courage and be respectful.

Within Explorers, I adhered to it all. Outside of it, I adhered to none. However much I enjoyed the place, I'd joined for one reason only – a reason that came up on our first joint camping trip with other groups in the neighbourhood. To get to Jarrod. My aim had been to befriend him and show him how much more pussy there was out there than boring old Melissa. Not that I expected he'd done much with her at fourteen. The only intimacy I'd ever witnessed was from Melissa - grabbing his hand, jumping up to kiss his cheek, and putting her arms around his neck and making him kiss her. Oh, he tried to get into it, I could tell, but he wasn't fully committed.

Though at that stage I hadn't known the *why*.


The first time I went to camp for the weekend, my scout group was one among a few from the locality, including Jarrod's group.

A treasure hunt set up for the Saturday daytime proved to be my way to get near to him. I found him sitting on the stump of a tree by himself. He wasn't distressed. If anything, he looked bored.

'Hey, do you live near Hendon Street?'

Jarrod looked up. I could see his face registering he knew me and trying to place where from. 'I don't. My girlfriend Melissa does.'

I pulled a thinking face. 'Ah, that's it,' I said. 'I asked for directions once, and you were very helpful. I remember you and your friend.'

'Thought you looked familiar,' he said, 'But I'd never have remembered that. You've got a good memory.'

'I have, and unfortunately, I remember how crap camp is.'

Jarrod tore off a piece of tall grass. 'Tell me about it.'

'Are you forced to come here too? My parents thought it would be good for me to meet people. They say I'm too "insular".'

He nodded. 'My dad is very religious. He's a scout leader. Insists I need to uphold his beliefs.'

'Is he here?'

'No. He hurt his back, so he stayed home, but *I've* still had to come.' Jarrod got up and kicked the tree stump. 'It fucking stinks here. They all bully me because I'd rather hang with the girls and the girls don't want to know me because of my dad. They say he's a pervert, you know?'

'Standard name calling for scout leaders or teachers that.'

'Yeah, well, it's not fair on me.' He looked at the floor.

'So I guess you're not doing the activity then?'

Jarrod looked at me as if I'd asked him if he was going to the moon. 'No chance. I'll just turn up at the meeting point. They expect me to be useless anyway.'

'I'm sure you're not. Look, how do you fancy going

round together? See if we're better as a team. I hate the kids in my own group.'

Jarrod tilted his head. 'I thought you said you were insular?'

'I usually am. But I must recognise you as being cut from the same cloth I am. There's an old saying for you.' I laugh.

'My dad talks like that. He's an idiot.'

'Well, he's no doubt expecting to hear you failed at the activity, so let's go and do our best. Let word get back to him that you aren't what he believes you are. Then I can go back and say I've made a friend and shock my own parents.'

He nods and follows me. He never was a challenge.


On the second camp, we acknowledged each other as we arrived. I got to see Jarrod's father. I overheard him calling his son a pansy and saying that he would stop him hanging around with Melissa unless he manned up.

It disgusted me to see him treated that way. Yet in front of everyone else, his father portrayed himself as a friend to all and holier than thou.

We met up where we could during the weekend. I found Jarrod easy to talk to. I looked forward to meeting up with him. He was completely transparent with me. Admitting to his weaknesses. No lies. No falsehoods. I told him so.

His face fell, and he looked on the verge of tears. 'Oh Edward. I'm sorry, but that's not true. I'm a walking web of lies.'

My forehead creased. 'I don't understand. Have you not been telling me the truth?'

Jarrod turned to face me with a look of sheer terror. 'I daren't tell you the truth, Ed. You'd hate me, and I couldn't bear for that to happen. You and Mel are all I have.'

I bristled at the mention of her name.

'You can tell me anything, Jarrod, anything at all.'

He began to cry. I couldn't bear it and pulled him into my arms. I couldn't explain it, but it felt right. I felt his suffering as if it poured from him and through my own skin.

'Not even Mel knows this,' he said.

Then he told me how he wished he'd been born female. He was attracted to Mel, but also found himself drawn to some men. That he didn't feel he really knew who he was. I had to hide the shock on my face. What he'd given me was the perfect story for revealing to Melissa. To take away her relationship. But I stared at the mixed-up teenager who had disintegrated into a ball of nothingness, not believing he had any worth and I realised I could build him up, make him stronger, make him who I wanted him to be. So I stroked his hair and reassured him that he was not alone. I confessed that I was adopted – that my whole world was a lie. I didn't tell him I was Melissa's brother. I wasn't that stupid. That weekend he looked up to me like you would a pop star or film star that you've made into your hero. He hung onto my every word as if I was the Lord himself.

On the third camp, when we escaped to the woods to talk, I made a move that could have killed my plans, but it was my last scout camp, and I needed to make progress. We'd been chatting for ages. He'd been telling about how he'd been dressing in Mel's clothes. How he felt guilty after.

'Why do you feel guilty for being you?' I asked him. 'You need to embrace who you are. If it has to be in secret for now, so be it. I'll keep your secrets. I'll always be your confidante.'

'I know I rarely get to see you, but I don't know what I'd do without you,' Jarrod had said. 'Just knowing when I lie in bed at night, that someone out there knows how I really feel. It helps, you know? If it weren't for you, Ed, I think I might have done something stupid by now.'

I pulled him towards me and wrapped my arms around him. 'You must never talk like that, Jarrod. You hear me? Being different does not mean you should have to conform to other people's versions of acceptable. You can always be yourself with me.'

'But I hardly see you. I wish you lived a bit nearer and that Melissa didn't get so jealous of other friends. I haven't told her about you, do you know that? How bad is it that I can't even be honest with her about making a good friend? She'd get jealous, so it isn't worth the hassle.'

'Then we'll stay a secret, and one day maybe it will be different.'

It's then I took the chance. I turned Jarrod's face to my own, leaned in, and kissed him.

Jarrod pulled his head back sharply and stared at me, anger displayed in his eyes, and tension in his jaw. Then he threw himself towards me, his lips back on my own, with an ardour I'd never experienced with any woman. I realised later, the anger he'd displayed was not at me, but the period of being at war with himself.

I backed him up towards the tree. Dusk was coming, and there was no one around. We didn't have long before we'd have others looking for us though. I pulled down his tracksuit bottoms and returned to kissing him. I wet my finger, having read about such things in the top shelf magazines passed around the classroom, and I pushed it up his arsehole. Jarrod arched towards me, his dick erect. Lowering myself to the ground, I took his cock in my mouth and sucked him until he erupted into my throat. It didn't take long.

When he cried afterwards, I licked up every tear. I told him I was sorry for doing it.

'No. Ed. You don't understand. I loved it. I felt things with you I've never felt with Mel. Almost everything I do with Mel is a lie. I'm so confused.'

I placed his hand around the girth of my own cock. 'Please.'

He pumped, tentative at first, and then his breath came harder until I came. I pulled out of his hand as I felt my balls tighten and sprayed cum against the tree.

'Meet me here again in the early hours of the morning. Please?' I begged.


He gave me his phone number and very occasionally, for the next year or so, we met up. We'd progressed to me fucking his anus while he pleasured me with his hand and mouth. He didn't want to take me the same way, and that was fine. We'd determined this was the way we fit best. I fell in love with him and begged him to move in with me when he turned eighteen.

'I can't,' he said with tears in his eyes. 'I'm going to marry Melissa.'

My heart shattered, and I placed barbed wire protection over it. Blocked him from my mind. Blocked out the words that said the world wasn't ready for us. We'd be beaten up. Spat at.

I told him I couldn't see him anymore, and with a final farewell fuck, he agreed that was how it had to be.

'I'll come for you,' I said. 'When the world has a better tolerance, I'll come for you. So don't do anything stupid.'

Yet it appears I only delayed what he would do anyway, years down the line. That bitch made him believe he'd lost me forever. Now he's in hospital, and it's her fault. Well, if she thinks we're done, she's a fool.

## CHAPTER TWENTY-FIVE

Edward

I'm exhausted. Adrenaline had pushed me to the hospital. Now I was fading fast. I needed to get to bed. Tomorrow, I would start afresh with my diet and strength building. Get back to the man I was before. I'd look into laser surgery for the tattoos too. Today, I admitted defeat. I needed my own bed.

'Christ, what's happening here, man?' the taxi driver mutters.

I look out of the front window and see people out of their doorways, standing on the pavement.

'Fire engine up ahead. Looks like a house fire,' he says.

I know before I get out of the taxi. I pay the driver and thank God I took some money out of the house and stuck it in my pocket. As I walk as near as the barricades will allow, I realise it's all I have left. The heat from the fire hits you from metres away.

A fireman approaches me. 'Keep back, mate. No one can go any closer. We've had to evacuate.'

'It's my house.'

I look towards Dave and Melissa's house as I wait. Their curtains are closed upstairs. Are they fucking while my house burns down? Are they celebrating that they won?

What is the loss of our home going to do for Inez's mental state?

With my details handed over to the fire brigade and a contact number taken, I make another call to a taxi firm and get taken to a hotel. Then I sleep until the phone interrupts me. It's the fire brigade with an update that the fire is out. Then I sleep again, my body wracked with exhaustion. I've paid for a week's stay at this budget hotel, added to my credit card. In the morning I'll phone work, make up some excuse as to where I've been and get back to my desk. I need to get earning again while we await the insurance on the house.

In the end, I decide to call into the office in person. I end up in a heated argument with Jack.

'No. I did not hand in my resignation. I assure you.'

'It came from your email address, Ed,' says Jack. 'I don't know what's going on with you and your wife, but you need time out. She was in here last week not making any sense either.'

'I didn't hand in my resignation. Someone else did.'

There's a pause. 'Someone broke into your house and used your computer to send a letter of resignation?' He shoves his hands in his pockets. 'You agree that sounds a bit weird, don't you? Unless... Was it Sam? Is it true you've had it away with her, you naughty boy? Whoa, bit Bunny Boiler her breaking into your home to do that. Or did you have her round while the missus was out shopping, you sly dog, Ed.'

I sigh. At least he's offered me a decent excuse. 'Yes, Sam probably did it. So can you destroy it? Can I come back to work?'

'Sure you can, mate.' He comes towards me and bumps shoulders. I want to push him into the wall. 'We'll have to get down Spearmint Rhino now I know you're one of the boys. Unless you're still with that Sam, you lucky bastard. Those tight thighs, fuck, I'd have liked those around my head.'

I endure ten more minutes of this before we agree I'll return to work on the following Monday. That's my job back. It's time to phone the insurance company so I can see about getting the house rebuilt.

'I'm sorry, Mr Bonham. A chip pan fire is excluded from your policy. You cannot claim on this occasion.'

I try so very hard to hold my temper, but my voice rises anyway. 'I've told the fire brigade. I didn't leave a pan on. I hadn't had anything to eat. I don't even eat chips.'

'Look, you'll have to take it up with them. We have their report. It states major damage to the kitchen and dining area, and the rest of the property is badly affected by heavy soot and smoke deposits on all surfaces. There's nothing more we can do from our end. Good day, sir.'

I throw a water glass at the wall where it sprinkles in shards. Before, only my stepmother made me lose control. Now *she* had. My *sister*. Now I had a fucking glass to pay for on top of house repairs if the fuckers didn't cough up. I pick up the shards one by one. Might as well put them to some use seeing as I'll have to pay for the glass. I wrap the shards in tissue and place them in my pocket.

She still has fucking everything. A loving husband that she's with because of me. Why did she never see it like that? Her ex-husband was not the route to her happiness. It was a fucked-up way, but she ended up with a husband who loved her, and stepchildren. But she still wasn't happy. I see the surly face of a young Mel in my mind. The one who didn't want to give me directions. She has no room in her life for anything not carefully considered. I guess in that way we're quite similar. Maybe it's a trait from our mother? I wouldn't know because Mel kept me from knowing her.

I mutter to myself. Shaking my head as I think things through.

*Tomorrow I get my car back.*

*Time for some visits.*

*Inez. I'm coming to see you, Inez. I'll bring my belt.*

I chuckle.

*Then sister dear, I'm coming to see you.*

I shake the shards in my pocket. I have just the idea.

## CHAPTER TWENTY-SIX

Melissa

The For Sale sign swings in the breeze outside our house. I'll be glad when someone purchases it, and we can be on our way. Far from here and from them. I don't know what's happening with Jarrod, Edward, or the house, and I honestly don't care. It's as if a huge weight has lifted from me. Our daughters found their stepmother's makeover strange, but they quickly came around. My grandchildren are adorable. I've missed so much. Jude is now fourteen. He's taller than I am. Becky also has a ten-year-old son called Marc. Today little Millie is here. She's Joanne's daughter and is three years old. She delights with her singsong voice and theatrical ways. I realise that we'd miss them so much if we moved to the States. Why should we miss out on time with our grandchildren? Haven't I missed enough? We need to stay nearer.

I'm making an apple pie when Millie runs in clutching a wrapped gift box.

'Millie. Where's that come from?' I laugh, assuming grandad is spoiling her once again.

'Man passed it through window.'

I drop the pie dish and snatch it from her hand. 'What man?'

She stands startled. Her lip wobbling and tears threatening.

'He said give you box. He said friend, Grandma.'

I clutch her towards my apron. 'I'm sorry, Millie. You did nothing wrong. The naughty man shouldn't have come to our window. He's still a stranger, okay? I'll lock the windows now. Don't go near him again if he comes back, Millie.'

'Okay, Grandma. What's in the box?'

'I'll look later.' I stuff the box in my apron pocket. 'Can you help me finish this pie?'

Thank goodness three-year-olds are easily distracted.

When the pie's in the oven and Millie is on the sofa

watching children's TV, I hover in the kitchen doorway and remove the box from my pocket. When I remove the lid, shards of broken glass are contained within. A gift tag says simply, 'Ed'. The message is clear. He gave my granddaughter broken glass. He's not finished. We're not safe.

I hate him. Why did he decide to ruin my life?

It's time to move. To escape. Also, it's time to seek answers.


We'll have no choice but to temporarily move to the house at Handforth. I don't know what I'll do with it going forward. Maybe I'll see if a developer wants to take a gamble on it? It's uninsurable, so I doubt it, but maybe they can make the surrounding area safe again? If not, I'll have to leave it behind. It reminds me too much of Edward now. This was my parents final home, but their happy place has been soiled by that man. He's like a slow spreading toxin. I need to know one way or another if we're related. For that, I'm going to need to see him again.

I'm going to get rid of this man once and for all.

But how?

## CHAPTER TWENTY-SEVEN

Edward

'Edward Bonham speaking.'

'You got your job back then?' Melissa's voice teases down the line. My hand tightens around the telephone.

'No thanks to you.'

'Thank you for the gift. If you ever pull a stunt like that with my granddaughter again, you'll be back at my house eating a cake with those very ingredients.'

'Is that why you're ringing, Melissa? To warn me off? Good to know I got to you.'

There's a sigh down the phone.

'No. I need to know something once and for all.

Can you give me your current address? I need to get something delivered to you.'

'I'm not sure about that. You'll forgive me for being suspicious.'

'It's a DNA test kit. I've been in touch with a company. Results within 24 hours for sibling tests.'

'Oh, in that case I'll definitely tell you. Can we meet for the results? I want to see your face.'

'How's my ex-husband doing?'

I stay silent.

'Oh, my God, he won't see you, will he?'

'Inez is a she, Mel. Can you get your head around that? Jarrod lived a lie.'

'Yeah, well he/she lived one with you too. Who knows who's coming out of that hospital.'

I tell her my address and hang up.


Two days later we arrange to meet in a cafe. Melissa has the results envelope in her hand. I watch as she walks toward me, her face devoid of any emotion.

'Lovely to see you again, sis. Have you missed me?'

'Save it, Edward.' She sits down and re-opens the envelope. 'Our score indicated that we are indeed half siblings.'

I clutch onto Melissa's arm and act like it's the best

news I've ever received. It isn't difficult because knowing what this will do to her, makes it some of the best news I've ever received.

Melissa gets up to leave.

'Where are you going, sis?'

She turns towards me. 'I'm going for a drink. Coffee won't do it for me today. I suggest you follow me. I want to know what this is about. What do you want so I can live my life without you in it?'

'That's not very sibling-like, is it?' I reply and then guffaw.

She orders a bottle of red wine. It's a good name, not the house crap and I tell her we'll share. We take a seat opposite each other next to the large windows of the bar. It gives me a sense of satisfaction that she chooses a public seat – shows me she's afraid of being in a dark corner with me. I have control. It makes my dick hard. Not for her. She'll never do that for me, bitch. But the power. The control. I realise how things could have gone very wrong if I'd have slept with Sam. She didn't know we were related and I didn't know she was Melissa. The thought makes me boil with anger. The stupid bitch.

Melissa sits back in her seat.

'So what is this about?' She sighs. 'I know you met and fell for Jarrod.' She sees my reaction. 'Sorry, Inez. You met and fell for *Inez* at explorers. She told me. Then you moved to the estate to what, win her back?'

'Yes, and to take her from you.'

'So, part of this was not undying love and devotion for my ex but the need to get at me. Why? What did I ever do to you?'

I take a sip of my drink. 'Our mother wouldn't acknowledge me because of you.'

'I don't understand.'

I fill her in on all the times I visited our mother. Melissa's face pales but flushes with the wine she consumes to cope with what she's hearing.

'Ed. You were born out of wedlock at a time people didn't accept those things.' She tries to reason. 'It wasn't me that stopped you being accepted. It was the time of your birth.'

'No. She told me. She wanted me in her life, but it would upset you too much, so she chose you over me. She gave me away to my adoptive parents and then rejected me again for you. Twice I wasn't good enough. I watched you. You had everything. Loving parents, a great family home, a best friend who became a boyfriend and then husband. I had an adoptive father who was never there and a mother who killed herself.

Then I got a stepmother with no morals. She knew me from my adoption as a baby and let me fuck her. Who in their right mind does that? You got the life that should have been *mine*,' I spit, droplets of red wine splash my chin.

Mel pulls at the top of her hair while she moves it away from her face. 'I am genuinely sorry that your life was not idyllic, but I can't apologise for being born, Ed. My mother made those choices – not me. She chose to have you adopted. She chose not to include you again.'

I realise then that it's Melissa who has the power. By seating us in a public place, I can't unleash my anger. Instead, I clutch the stem of my glass so hard, I fear it may break off in my hand.

'You're not the only one whose life was a lie, Edward. That's the joke in all of this. My *idyllic*'— she makes speech quotes with her fingers around the word –'life, was based on a mother who hid from me, and maybe even my father, that she had another child. And with them both deceased I have no way of asking either of them what the truth is. So you see, you've taken my so-called happy childhood and ruined it for me forever. Well done.' She slow hand-claps. 'As for my friend and boyfriend, well we all know how that turned out. Years of lies. You're not the only person who would like a do-over.'

She sits back and laughs. 'I was about to say that I wish I'd never met Jarrod, but I'd still have had you in my life, wouldn't I? Ready to destroy whatever path I'd have trodden. Did you ever love him? Or was it just to get back at me?'

'It started as getting back at you. I was going to steal your friend. That was all. But he showed me his true self, and I genuinely fell for him. I didn't try to make him something he's not.'

'Is that so? Because you named him Inez and you never let him make any decisions. That doesn't sound like someone who fell in love. You never let Jarrod be who he wanted to be.'

She puts her glass down on the table. 'That's why he's not seeing you, isn't it? You want Inez back, but he's not Inez anymore, is he?'

The bitch is clever. 'No. And that's down to you. You took him away from me.'

'Right back at you. Karma's a bitch.' She snorts.

'Are you happy with Dave, Melissa?'

She bristles at the mention of his name. 'Don't bring him into this.'

'But he's already involved, isn't he? He's part of the whole sordid evening. What happened that night, Melissa? What was it like when they took the foetus from your body. Was it already dead?'

I knock my wine over purposefully and the red spills over Melissa's top. She looks down at the blood red stains.

Tears spill down her face. I've never seen her weak, and it's glorious. I want to lick the tears from her face and rejoice in the salty taste on my tongue.

She takes a deep inhale and exhale. 'I won't answer those sick questions except to say that I could cope with your stealing Jarrod. I could have coped with finding out I had a brother. I would have welcomed you.' She mops at her stomach with a tissue. 'I always wanted a sibling. I used to nag my parents to death for one. I'd have loved you. But the evening of the accident, when I was hit by a taxi, you left me half-dead. Neither of you came up to help. I've never recovered from my loss and I never will. I'm happy with Dave. I truly am. My grandchildren are beautiful inside and out. But they'll never be mine. You took away the opportunity to do what I'd yearned for my whole life. To give life. I was so excited to meet my baby and then when I did-' She stops and cries again.

I wait until she composes herself.

'Are you the slightest bit regretful about what happened, Edward? Do you wish things could have been different?'

'No.' I tell her honestly. 'I wish I could bottle every tear on your face.'

'You sick fuck,' she spits.

I laugh. 'Oh, sister, there's so much more about me you need to know. Like, I'm not done. You're happy again, and I'm not. So, what's it to be? You help me get my wife back, or I make sure you don't have a husband – again.'

She throws the remainder of her glass of wine in my face. I wonder what anyone watching us is thinking?

I lick drops of wine off my lips. 'I wonder what Dave's blood would taste like?'

'You disgust me.'

I laugh and shrug my shoulders.

She sits back down. 'What do you want me to do?'

I leave the pub with a great sense of satisfaction. Looks like things are going my way again. I head to the rental property I've leased for myself and Inez when she returns. Work let me have an advance on my wages so I could get back on my feet. Inez will love the house. It's around the corner from our old home, and the layout of the property is the same. I've paid a deposit on a new puppy, the exact breed and look as Bounty. Everything will be back to normal soon. Once home, I get my gym kit out ready for the morning and place it on the chair at the end of the bed. I can restart my gym activities now I'm gaining strength and know I'm unlikely to be kidnapped again. Not if my dear sister Mel values that family of hers.

## CHAPTER TWENTY-EIGHT

Melissa

Dave's face reddens. His eyes protrude and a vein pulses in his forehead. 'He's never going to leave us alone then, is he? The man's psychologically disturbed. We've no chance against him. So let's just cut our losses and disappear.'

I shrug. 'And how do we explain that to the children? There's no way they are going to uproot everyone.'

He paces. 'What about the police?'

I look down at the floor. 'I think I'd have a lot of explaining to do.'

He runs his hands through his hair. 'God, this is such a mess.'

'Yes, well, having split them up, I now face having to get them back together again. What the fuck was any of the past few years for?' I throw a cushion at the wall, because I'm so damn frustrated, but I don't want to break anything. 'You're better off without me, Dave. I should have never come home.'

'No.' He rushes towards me, places his arms around my body. 'Then he's won. We'll think of a way, Mel. We will. We need him gone.'

I break away from him and sit in front of the computer and begin to type furiously.

'What are you doing?'

'I'm seeing if I can find any Bonham's in the area near to where I used to live when I was a teenager,' I tell him. 'It's a long shot but worth a try. Oh, my God, there's an I. Bonham. Do you think it could be a relation?'

'There's only one way to find out,' answers Dave with a weary sigh.

The next day I'm off to a nearby neighbourhood of my old haunts to see an Inez Bonham. I'm entirely fascinated by the fact that she has the same name Ed gave

Jarrod. He said he shagged his stepmother, but wow, this is really fucked up. She wouldn't be drawn into any conversation on the phone, saying she wanted to meet me face to face.

I enter the block of four grey concrete coated flats. They look dilapidated, and as I open the door, the smell of stale piss fills the air. I ring the doorbell of the number Inez gave me and wait. A few minutes later the door opens. A grey-haired lady who looks to be in her mid-seventies opens the door. Her eyes fix on mine, her gaze sharp.

'Come in, Melissa.'

'How did you know—?'

'No one else visits, dear.' She strolls back down the hall.

I'm invited into a stark living room. It has a sofa that's seen better days and a wooden chair. There's a radio on the side, but I note there's no television. A newspaper on a coffee table at the side of the chair is open at a crossword, a pen lying on the paper. Inez's gait is strong for her age, and it would appear her mind is the same.

'I actually hoped I'd never hear Edward's name again. It's been years now. I thought I was free. Sorry, I'm being rude. Would you like a drink of tea?'

'No. I'm fine thank you.' I hover near the doorway.

'Actually, if we're talking about Edward, then sherry's probably more appropriate.' She passes me to go into the kitchen and returns with a bottle and two glasses. It looks like I'm having a drink whether I want one or not.

She sits on the sofa, then pours and passes me a small glass of sherry, nodding towards the chair. 'So, what brings you here?'

I take a seat. 'As I explained on the phone. My name is Melissa, and I've recently found out that Edward is my brother.'

'Let me guess. That's disturbed you. He's disturbed you?'

'It's a lot more complicated than that.' I tell her about Jarrod. I leave out that I kidnapped Ed. I let her know that he's obsessed and won't leave me alone.

'Oh dear.' Inez takes a sip of sherry. 'I know what that's like. It used to be me.'

I take a swallow before I speak. 'Edward said that you and he were lovers?'

Inez sighs. 'Oh, that old chestnut's back, is it?' She shakes her head.

'You mean you weren't?'

'No. We weren't. I was his stepmother, and I loved his father dearly. Edward had problems right from being around three years old. He exhibited very strange behaviour. Quite obsessional compulsive at times. Everything in his room had to be a certain way. He had to do things in a particular order. If not, he'd have a meltdown. His adoptive father worked away a lot, and he was left with his mother. No one realised the stress it put on her until it was too late. She took an overdose. Left a note saying the stress of caring for Edward was too much.'

'So she didn't do it because her husband cheated?'

'No. He didn't cheat.'

'He said you were the social worker who arranged his adoption.'

The corner of her mouth upturns. 'I was. Lucky me, eh? After Ed's mother died, Ed's father, William, came to see us. I was still working in the same department. He wanted to know if we could help with Edward. The department couldn't, but I became involved - too involved, and in the end, we married, and I became Ed's stepmother. His behaviour got worse. He was in and out of psychiatric units. He told them I'd slept with him. That led to quite intrusive investigations as you can imagine. He couldn't come home after that. He had to be fostered. Foster parents couldn't cope with him either. He ended up in care homes when he wasn't having psychiatric treatment. He's never changed his story though. He's convinced we had a relationship. It broke me and his father up in the end as the doubt was always in William's mind. There shouldn't be any doubt in a relationship, should there? There should only be trust.'

The sadness is etched on Inez Bonham's face. She clearly loved Ed's father, and yet it wasn't strong enough to survive Edward Bonham.

'When did you last see Ed?'

'Gosh, not since the late eighties. He came to see me to tell me he'd met someone. Couldn't stop going on about them. Said he knew it was meant to be. That was all he'd tell me. Not even a name. Anyway, after that, he left me alone. To be honest, I didn't care. His obsession with me was over, just like that.' She snaps her fingers.

'I'm afraid it wasn't,' I tell her. I tell her about Edward making Jarrod into Inez.

It makes me regretful of coming here when I see her tremble. 'Oh, dear God. I thought it was over.'

'The thing is,' I tell her. 'Inez is in a psychiatric ward being evaluated. It's all got too much. Now Ed wants me to get her back for him. I don't know where this will end. When is he going to leave us alone?'

Inez fixes me with those eyes of steel. 'When his obsession moves on, or when he's dead.'

We're quiet as I drink the rest of my sherry.

She asks me to excuse her for a moment and then returns from the room she had gone to. She hands me a piece of paper with an address and phone number on it.

'If you need me I'll be here,' she says pointing to the piece of paper. 'It's my niece's house. She always annoying me about going to stay. I don't feel safe here now. If that ex of yours doesn't go back to him, I don't know what Ed will be capable of. I'm not going to stay around to find out. I'm too old for his shit. I want to see my last days out in peace. Please don't let him get hold of this information.'

'I won't. He won't know I've been here. Thank you for seeing me. I'm sorry to bring up old memories.'

'When you have Edward in your life you're never completely free of looking over your shoulder.'

I nod, and after thanking her for the drink, I leave the house.

The next thing on mine and Dave's agenda is to get packed for the move to Handforth. We take the For Sale sign down on our house and take it off the market for a short time. That way, if Edward makes enquiries, he'll think we've changed our mind. Instead, we're escaping to my parents' old home until we can make plans to move. We only need to pack clothes and essentials as the house is furnished and has everything we need. A food shop and we'll be sorted. I take clean bedding. We fill up the car, and we're on our way.

Dave has never been to the house before, though he knew of it. We pull up outside. The weather today is dismal. It's been raining for days, and the uneven ground is full of puddles.

I pull my hood up and clutch my coat tighter around me. 'Come have a look around inside first, then we'll unpack.'

He nods.

I take him through the front door. The house is in dire need of decoration but is clean. From the small hallway, I show Dave through to the lounge. It's a long narrow room with an old wooden circular dining table at one end, complete with matching chairs with threadbare cushion pads.

'Gosh, it's like going back in time.' He laughs.

'It is. I never saw the point in spending money on it when it's virtually worthless.'

Dave looks out of the back window. 'So, the other houses are worthless?'

'Yes, and they're derelict after years of being left to rot. Roof tiles came off, windows cracked. The rain leaked in. I'm not sure if my house is entirely safe, but

I've seen no signs of damp, so I've always assumed it's okay.'

'You little risk-taker you.' He laughs. 'We'd better take it steady in the bedroom. I don't want to bring the house down.' He winks.

He walks through to the kitchen giving it a cursory glance and then moves into the downstairs study where I hear him gasp. I follow him into the room, and my eyes follow his. I note him taking in the chain dangling from the wall. The tattoo equipment that remains in the room.

'What on earth happened here?'

'You don't need to know, but from what's here I'm sure you can guess.'

He moves to the window and sees the rectangular hole.

'Dug for psychological purposes only. I wasn't that hell bent on revenge.'

'The chain though.' He looks back at the wall. 'You kept him chained?'

'While I tried to destroy him, yes,' I bite out. 'Wasn't going to work very well trying to reason with him.'

'It's a shock, that's all. I'm not criticising. I'm trying to imagine this new side to my wife. I may have to get a tattoo.'

I smile. 'Would you really let me tattoo you?'

'I would trust you with my life.'

'And what would you have me etch on you?'

'A chameleon,' he says without hesitation. 'To remind me of you.'

I laugh. 'A chameleon? Is that what I am?'

'Yes.' He drags me to him. 'The outside of you changes but inside.' He strokes my breast. 'Is the same woman I've always known, deep down. You adapt to your surroundings.' He begins to move out of the room. 'Tomorrow I'll fetch some filler and paint, and we'll give the study a little redecoration. Maybe you could fill that hole in the garden? It creeps me out.'

I shake my head. 'What a wuss. Come on, I'll show you the bedroom.'

The bedrooms are the only rooms I changed after my parents' deaths. New furniture and redecorated rooms that I did myself. I had taken the back bedroom for my own. I'd kept Ed in the front bedroom, and this would need to be cleaned out. I didn't want a trace of him left in that room. The bedrooms had to be changed as I didn't want to be reminded of my parents being sick and ill. They'd died within such a short space of time of each other, my father from leukaemia and my mother through a fall that led to pneumonia, though I'd say it was a broken heart that claimed her really. And she'd taken her secret to the grave. Never admitting to me at any point in her life that there was something I didn't know. Then a thought comes to me unbidden. The Solicitor stating that my mother had left some money to a charity, but she wanted it to be anonymous to everyone. It struck me as odd at the time as she'd never particularly donated anywhere. Had it really been to charity or had she left something to Ed? Had she lied to me even after death?

'Are you alright?' Dave's voice breaks through. I realise I've been sitting on the edge of the bed lost in my own thoughts for some minutes.

'I will be. I hope. It's knowing that every aspect of my childhood and life up to losing my baby was based on lies, Dave.'

He nods.

'None of it was how it appeared. It feels like a waste of all those years of my life.'

Dave places his arm around me. 'Mel. Were you happy? When you were living with your parents, and you had Jarrod. Right up until it went wrong. Were you happy?'

'Yes,' I tell him. 'My life felt perfect.'

'Then that's all that matters,' he assures me. 'You felt loved, and you were happy. No matter what came after. At the time of your childhood and young adulthood, you had health and happiness. Yes, people kept secrets. Most of us have secrets. Skeletons in cupboards.'

'Did you have a secret when you were younger?' I ask him.

'I did,' he says but adds nothing further.

I bump him with my hip. 'Tell me.'

'No.' He smirks.

I twirl my hands in his hair, 'I'll make it worth your while.'

He looks down at me. 'When I was in my late twenties, a young woman moved in across the street. Now, I was happily married with two young children, but hey, I wasn't blind. When she came to our house to get cooking lessons from my first wife, I used to try and sneak a peek down her top because her nipples used to show through her blouse. I used to imagine sticking her breasts in my mouth instead of the buns she used to offer me.'

'Is that right?' I ask him, removing my top to reveal my bra. Then I pull my bra down to reveal a breast.

'Were they like these?'

'Smaller, but I'm sure I can get just as excited at imagining these in my mouth,' he tells me.

And he does.

. . .

The following day is a Saturday, and Dave busies himself fixing the study and the wall of the front bedroom. We keep the windows open all day, despite the continuing rain, to let fresh air in and the smell of paint out. I clean and dust as if I can wipe out all traces of Edward having been in this house.

At one point, we break off for coffee and cake. I watch as Dave finishes eating but continues to chew his lip.

'What?'

'I don't quite know how to ask this, but it's bugging me.'

'So ask.'

'Bobby,' he says. 'You spent years with him. Was there ever anything between you?'

I stare at the lines of grief etched on my husband's face, so visible to me right now with the light cast from the window. He's spent all these years imagining the worst.

'You'll have to meet Bobby sometime. You'll like him. He's a character. But since we got together, there has never been anyone but you.' I move over to him and sit at his feet. 'There never will be, as far as I'm concerned, anyone but you.'

'There was Jarrod again. The video,' he says.

'I barely tolerated that. It made me sick to my stomach, but I had to do it. Do you understand that? I did what I had to do for the video, and I've regretted it ever since. I felt soiled.'

'But that's the point I'm trying to make, Mel. If it comes to it, for revenge, again, would you do it?'

'No.' I reach up and caress his lip. 'I only want you. Only you, Dave.' I undo the fly of his trousers and take him in my mouth, vowing to worship his body until the day he believes me again because right now he doesn't trust me and I don't trust myself.

I think back to the original Inez Bonham's words. *There shouldn't be any doubt in a relationship, should there? There should only be trust.*

I need to know that's what Dave and I have, and we can only have that if Edward is no longer in our lives.

## CHAPTER TWENTY-NINE

Inez

I've been having counselling, and I'm feeling so much better. Of course, I've not been able to talk about everything that's happened the past few years, but I've been able to discuss my feelings about not living the life I want. Ed is coming to visit today. I phoned him. Told him I wanted to chat. I've been told I can be discharged when I have a place to go and so I'm going to talk to Ed and see if I'm able to come home.

When he walks through the door at visiting time he looks weary. He approaches me, but where he would normally place his arms around me and gather me to him, he's hesitant. I don't blame him.

'Take a seat,' I say.

We're in the day room. A small room with large windows to one side that faces the industrialised city. There are a few nondescript chairs, a coffee table, and a television set.

Ed takes a seat at the side of me.

'How have you been?' he asks.

'I'm feeling a lot better.' I smile at him. 'They say I can come home. That's why I've asked you here. I need to tell you how I'm feeling now and see whether you want me back.'

'Inez-'

'No'. I put my palm up. 'My name is Lynne now.'

'The house was badly damaged in a fire.'

I place a hand to my mouth. 'What?'

'It needs thousands of pounds' worth of repairs. The fire brigade and insurers are insisting it was my fault, that I left a pan on, but I know I didn't. It would take all my savings to repair the house. All of them. She's fucked my life up properly.'

'No. We fucked her life up,' I answer.

His jaw tightens and his eyes narrow, but he stays silent. 'I've rented a place around the corner from our house. It's furnished. It's obviously not our house, but it's the same layout. I hope you'll come back to me, Inez.'

'My name is-'

'Stop it,' he yells, spittle flying from his mouth. 'You're Inez to me. That's all you have been. Please, if you need to change, can you give me some time?' He puts his head in his hands. I wait while he focuses, calming himself down. He peers back at me. 'I'm coming to terms with what that woman has done to us. Can we go to our new home and be us – the normal us – for a little while? Then we'll talk about who you want to be. I can't handle this right now. I can't.'

I nod. Then I bite my own lip. I'm the same subservient person I've always been. He orders me, and I obey. That's the reality of my life. I may as well accept it. I have no backbone. But no matter how controlling he is, I love him.

'Let's go home,' I tell him.


Ed is worrying me. I hear him muttering to himself as he walks around the house.

The place might have the same room formation, but with its dirty and broken furniture, it's not our comfortable home. I bought cleaning materials and did the best I could to clean the place up, but it's not the same.

I fix us an evening meal, and we sit at the small table. I have questions that feel like they want to burst out of me and I decide to ask them. Ed can only refuse to answer.

'How did Melissa capture you?'

His eyes narrow. 'She had a bloke helping her. The same one who tried to knock my work reputation. They knocked me out. Next thing I knew I was in a house in the middle of nowhere.'

'It sounds like her house at Handforth.'

'I don't know where I was. I wasn't conscious to see my entrance, and I was blindfolded for my exit. I had an occasional view out of the window.'

'Were there other cottages nearby, but in ruins?'

'I don't know. There were never any other signs of life, and the view from the window was the garden and then dirt.'

'It sounds like her parents' home. They left it to her when they died.'

For some reason this makes Ed clutch his plate so hard, the end of his fingers turn white. 'It's her parents house? She took me there? She tortured me in the family home? Oh, my God. She put me in the bed. Was it my mother's bed?'

'What are you talking about, Ed?'

'Melissa. I wanted to tell you but I couldn't until she'd suffered. I knew you'd try to protect her. She's my half-sister. Her mother had me out of wedlock, shoved me to one side, then had Mel and lived happily ever after.'

'You're lying.'

He backhands me across the face. I jolt back in my seat and put my hand on my cheek where it smarts.

'I do not lie.' Ed's face is mottled, his eyes wide, showing the whites of his eyes. I've never seen him like this.

'I- I'm sorry, I'm just, um, confused. Don't forget all that's happened lately. You've brought me home from a psychiatric ward, Ed. You'll have to forgive me if I'm questioning everything around me.'

He falls to his feet and grasps my hands. 'I'm so sorry. I never should have struck you. Please, forgive me, Inez. I love you.'

I nod and stroke the top of his hair. Why am I comforting him when I'm the one who got hurt?

When we go to bed, Ed wants to get close, intimate, but I tell him I'm not ready for that yet. He leaves the bedroom, and I hear a banging noise downstairs. I daren't see what's happening, so I lie in bed until the night turns dark and Ed comes back up and goes to sleep. Only then do I feel I can close my own eyes. The next day I find pieces of a dining room chair outside, and chunks of plaster out of the wall.

While Ed is at work today, I'm going shopping. I've agreed for him to call me Inez still, but I want to explore a different look again. I laugh as I realise I miss my friend Selma. She'd have advised me on what to buy. Then I shake my head. No. I tell myself. This is about you, and what you want. For God's sake decide for yourself.

I cook Ed's favourite meal for dinner, shepherd's pie, and wait for him to come home.

When he walks into the dining room that night, he stares at me as if I've grown an extra head. I'm wearing a new ash-blonde wig in a layered bob shape. It appears so much more natural than the long dark wig. I visited the makeup counter again, and they were very patient with showing me how to apply my makeup. I look a lot more how I'd always imagined myself. With a pair of grey wide-legged trousers and a white blouse, I still have a classy look in the style Ed always asked of me, but I've made it my own.

'What the hell's going on?' he growls.

My forehead creases. 'I'm not sure what you mean. Pull up a chair, I made your favourite, shepherds pie.'

He stalks towards me. 'Well, perhaps it's not my

favourite anymore, *Lynne.*' Sarcasm drips from his lips when he says my new name. Perhaps I've decided on a change too?'

He grabs hold of the back of my neck with venom. His fingers pinch the top of my backbone. 'Has my money bought this shit?' he bellows. 'Last I knew, you weren't working. We're fucking skint, you silly bitch. You can take that back tomorrow. You look a complete cunt in it anyway. Where's the brown one?'

I wince under the pressure of his fingers. 'In the bedroom, in the chest of drawers.'

'Go and get it,' he snarls. 'Put it back on your head and remember that while we're together, you're Inez, and you have fucking brown hair, do you understand?'

He stands there while I remove my wig, then he rubs it through the shepherds pie, picking both up and throwing the lot on the floor. 'I'm going out,' he tells me. 'When I get back, this lot better not be here anymore. Make sure everything, including you'— he stabs his finger into my chest –'is back to normal.'

Then he grabs his car keys from the side and with a bang of the door is gone.

I slump onto a dining chair, clutching my head. Who the hell am I living with? There is none of the kind, loving husband I've lived with for all these years. The man who supported me through my change.

Whatever Mel did to him, she's changed him. Are they really siblings or did she break his mind like she broke mine?

I need to see her. To ask her the truth. If she's back with Dave, then she's only around the corner. Tonight, I will tidy up, put my brown wig back on and play the game. Tomorrow I'll see Mel and seek the answers that will either mend my relationship with Ed or finish it forever.

Once I've tidied up I go into my bag and take out my phone. I study a couple of selfies of us and some other photos of Ed. I'm grateful Mel didn't delete the ones of me and my husband. After the fire, I have no other pictures of us. I stare at the man in the photos. The man I love. Or, the man I loved? Who is the stranger I've come to live with and is my husband ever coming back?

## CHAPTER THIRTY

Edward

Locks are so easy to break. If someone doesn't come to the door, well then, I'll just let myself in. I take note of the storage boxes and the suitcase.

'Going somewhere, stepmummy?' I ask her.

She sits back against the headboard, rubbing her eyes. Her skin as white as a sheet of plain paper. Ready to be doodled on. I laugh.

'It's been years, Edward,' she says. 'Why now? Why are you here now? Are you not back with your wife?'

How the fuck does she know about my wife? God,

that bitch. Mel must have been here too. Interfering fucking cunt.

'That's the thing,' I say, withdrawing my belt from my trousers, 'I've lost my Inez. But then again, she never was you.'

She reaches over and switches on the light. It brings her lined face into focus. Her grey hair.

'Where's Inez?' I demand. 'You look like her. Are you her mother?' I begin to pace the room.

She gets out of bed and comes towards me.

'Edward. Look at me. You're ill again. It's me. I am your stepmother. I'm old now, Edward.'

'You lie,' I spit. What the hell is going on here? This is the address I've had in my mind for ages, recorded there. The address of Inez Bonham. 'Where's my stepmother?' I grab her throat.

'I am your stepmother,' she croaks out.

I drop my hold and look around. 'Inez has long dark hair, she's slim. We're lovers. She likes me to hurt her with this belt.'

'Edward,' the woman shouts. 'That never happened. How many more times do we have to go through this?'

I open wardrobe doors, searching for a clue as to the whereabouts of my stepmother. When I turn around, I see the phone in the old woman's hand.

'Oh no. I can't have you ringing anyone. Who are you phoning? Mel? Has she put you up to this? Are you her puppet?'

'No.' The old woman is crying now. 'I'm phoning my niece. I'm going to stay with her. That's why I'm packed. I'm letting her know she can fetch me now.'

I hold the belt up, wrapped around both of my fists.

'Oh no, sorry, you're going nowhere. Not until I find Inez,' I tell her. Then I take the phone from her hand.

## Inez

Ed doesn't speak to me when he gets home from work. In fact, he won't even look me in the eyes. He goes in the shower, changes into pyjamas, and then gets into bed. All night he mumbles my name, 'Inez'. I'm causing him pain, but I have to create more of a life for myself. I no longer want to be Inez Bonham. I know I'm changing. I'm so scared of the future. But I want to decide on my own appearance, not be told how to look. It's happened all my life. No more. Tomorrow morning, I will shop and replace the wig he destroyed. Lack of money or not. I will not lose this fight.

Ed is sombre at the breakfast table and unusually for him is not getting ready to go to the gym. I don't think he's entirely himself since his captivity. When he's a little calmer, I wonder if I might bring up the subject of counselling. He could have some psychological problems from being kidnapped.

'Could you pass me the milk please, Lynne?' he asks.

My eyes shoot up to meet his, but he's still not looking at me. Has he really come around to me choosing my name? That would be tremendous.

'You called me Lynne? Not Inez,' I say quietly.

'There's no more Inez,' he states, and picks up the newspaper from the table and opens it, separating our faces.

## CHAPTER THIRTY-ONE

Melissa

It makes the local news the next day. I'm on the internet when the post is shared on my feed.

**Witnesses sought in suspicious death of widow.**

It goes on to say how Inez Bonham had been found strangled at her house. I run to the bathroom where I lose all my breakfast. Dave is at work. It's got to have been Ed. Got to have been. I pace the bathroom trying to calm myself down. It will be a botched robbery. Nothing to do with Ed at all. I think of Jarrod. My God. Is he safe? I wanted revenge. I don't want him dead.

I reach for my phone.

'That's so strange, I was going to call around to see you today. Only Ed is saying the strangest things. He's saying he's your brother.'

There's no way I'm admitting to being the sister of a potential murderer unless I'm forced to.

'Inez.'

'I go by Lynne now.'

I pause. 'Good for you. Listen, Lynne. I don't know how else to say this, and with everything that's happened I don't expect you to trust me, but I have to try.'

I take a deep breath.

'Go on.'

'I don't think you're safe with Ed. They've just found his stepmother dead in her apartment, strangled.'

There's a loud laugh. 'I know he's controlling, but that hardly makes him a murderer.'

'His stepmother's name is, was, Inez Bonham. In her youth, she was slim and tall with long dark hair.'

'You're lying.'

'I don't expect you to believe me, but I met her. Edward was convinced they'd had a love affair. He was obsessed with her.'

'He loves me.'

'I agree, and I think he does, in his own strange way. I think you were a surprise he didn't expect in his life. But he's sick in the head. He's been in hospitals, and now his stepmother is dead. It's too much of a coincidence. How has he seemed to you?'

Inez sighs. 'Quiet. Mumbling'. There's a pause. 'A short temper. Oh, my God.'

'What? Lynne, what?'

'This morning. He said there's no more Inez. You don't think...?'

'All I know is that I don't think you're safe right now. Pack some belongings and get a taxi up to the house at Handforth. I've a spare room. We'll work out what to do.'

'I-' She hesitates.

'Forget everything from the past right now. I want a life. I can't have one while he's in it. Get here and then we need to phone the police. If he's innocent they'll let him go, won't they? No harm done. If he's not, you're safe here.'

'I'll be there as soon as I can.'

## Edward

I get home, and there's no food on the table.

No wife.

No Inez. My glorious Inez who I've adored all my life isn't here. My mind tries to fix on an image of her face, but it morphs into different ones.

I walk into the bathroom and realise her toothbrush has gone. I take the room apart. Some of her belongings are missing.

'Where the fuck is she?' I shout.

I sit on the floor and rock. I can't get my mind to hold a thought. I look at my hands, imagine them looping a belt around her neck. But that was an old woman, not Inez, wasn't it?

I couldn't concentrate at work today. Jack said they might have to let me go. So before I left, I hung him by his tie in the men's bathroom. That shut him up.

I pick up my mobile. Silly me. How could I have

forgotten? I put a tracker on my wife's phone so that I always knew where she was.

I wait until it shows me her location.

Well, well. A little house in Handforth. What are the chances of that?

Looks like we're going to be having a family reunion.

## CHAPTER THIRTY-TWO

Melissa

We call the police, and a detective constable is sent to us. It's a long time since another car came down the long winding lane to my house.

'Gosh. I didn't know anyone still lived down here,' the DC says, his eyes taking in his surroundings.

'That's because they don't,' I tell him in clipped tones. 'We're only here because it's safe from Edward.'

The DC records the details we give him. That Edward is unstable. That he had a fixation with his stepmother, who has been found dead. That we have no proof he's involved, but it's worth investigating. I tell him that he gave our granddaughter glass shards through the window.

To my surprise, Lynne is open about being my ex-husband and having gender reassignment. She re-iterates that Ed was obsessed with his stepmother and groomed her to look similar, although she was unaware that this was his intention.

'Okay. Well, I'll head back to the station with this. We need to pick up Edward and bring him in for questioning.' The DC gets up.

'As I said, he'll either be at the gym or at home, as that's where he goes from work,' says Lynne.

'Thank you. We'll be in touch.'

'What happens now?' Lynne asks. Her name is giving me a headache. I want to call her Jarrod or Inez. Though who am I to talk?

An hour or so later I move to the kitchen to make a drink. Sitting around is not doing me any good. I feel edgy and jumpy. The atmosphere in the house is tense with Lynne there with Dave. The last time they met Dave beat her up. The sooner they pick up Edward, the better. I'm not religious as a rule, but I pray to God that he's arrested for murder or at the very least taken for psychological assessment. I move to the sink to fill the kettle, but movement at the periphery of my vision has me startle.

The hairs on the back of my neck stand up as I stare at Ed on the other side of the window with a knife in his hand.

I scream and run for the lounge.

'Call the police. He's here.'

Dave quickly grabs the phone.

Lynne jumps up. 'How the hell did he know where we were?'

'I don't know,' I snap. 'He never saw the route when I brought him here.'

Lynne bites her lip. 'I told him you had property at Handforth. I'm sorry.'

I look at her in dismay. 'Sorry's a bit late when your psychopath husband is outside the kitchen window.' The last of my words are drowned out by the sound of glass shattering.

'He's trying to get in,' I shout.

Lynne runs through the lounge door and into the kitchen.

'What are you doing?' I yell.

'Barricade yourselves upstairs. I'm going out to him,' she says.

I look at Dave, his brow furrowed. 'Let's get upstairs to the toolkit. Grab what you can. Screwdrivers, hammer. Anything we can use to keep him at bay,' he says.

We scurry upstairs and dash into the spare room where there are tools from the recent redecoration.

I hear voices from outside and walk over to the bedroom window. Lynne's outside now, talking to Edward. He's waving a knife around. She holds her hands up. I can only hear mumbling but can see she's trying to get through to him.

'What on earth was she thinking?' says Dave.

'She doesn't think. Just acts. That's always been my ex's problem. Now we wait to see who gets to us first. The police or Edward.'

Once again, my ex's actions could destroy my life.

## Lynne

I couldn't sit there and wait for the police. Edward has loved me for all these years. He wouldn't hurt me. I feel it deep down inside. Whatever has happened, there must be an explanation.

'Edward, darling. Put the knife down, and we can talk.' I put my own hands up. 'Look. I don't have anything. It's just me. Inez.'

He waves the knife. 'But you're not, are you?

You're tricking me. I don't know what's happening. I picked up the signal of my wife's phone, and it brought me here. You look like her, but you don't.' He rubs his knife-free hand through his hair, agitated. Then he hits himself in the forehead. 'I can't remember what she looks like. I see long dark hair, but then I see an old woman. Then I see your face, but you're different.'

'You made me wear a wig. I have a different one on now. But this is me. Look.' I slowly remove the wig to reveal my own hair underneath.

'My Inez had proper long dark hair. It wasn't a wig. You're tricking me. Why? You want me to go back there, don't you? To that kid's unit. They held me down. I won't be held down. Where is my wife?' He lunges, and the knife slashes the skin on my arm. It hurts like a bitch. He's startled to see the blood, and while he's still, I turn and run back into the house holding the door closed. When he comes to, he kicks and thumps the back door.

'Let me in. I want my wife. What have you done with my wife?'

I find it harder and harder to keep the door closed and then there's nothing. A reprieve? Is he trying to fool me that he's gone? Then I see his shadow at the window and hear him picking pieces of broken glass from the frame. Oh shit.

Then the strangest experience occurs. The house shakes. At first, it's a small tremble. Then it stops, and for a brief moment, I think I imagined it. Then it starts again. Items fall off the tops of the kitchen cupboards. I hold onto the door, but it's like the kitchen floor is suddenly made of liquid. It seems to ripple. What the hell?

Mel and Dave rush downstairs. 'Lynne. We need to get out. It's not safe. Something's happening to the ground.' I hear the front door open, and I know I should move, but it's like I'm frozen to the spot. I watch as Ed tries to climb through the window and then suddenly he's not there anymore. As the ground stops trembling again, my senses are alert. Adrenaline pumps and I run out of the front of the house as fast as I can.

## CHAPTER THIRTY-THREE

Melissa

We ran as fast as we could to the houses at the top of the street, Lynne closely behind. A paramedic checks us over and places some paper stitches on a cut on Lynne's arm. The police come to meet us. They tell me my garden is no longer there, and neither is the back part of my home. The noise has brought out the ambulance chasers and other nosy residents of the local area. I overhear their mumbles.

'No ones lived there for years. They should have knocked them down long ago.'

'My kids play down there. Could have been there when it happened. Wonder if I could sue?'

We're advised to get in the police car, and leave them all to it.

Later a detective fills us in. 'It would appear that heavy rain caused an old mine shaft to collapse. The safety of the area is being determined. Mrs Bonham, you say that your husband is somewhere in that shaft, but at approximately ninety metres deep, that will take some time to determine. We also have staff working at the crime scene of the deceased Mrs Inez Bonham to see if we can find any evidence to connect Edward Bonham with her death.'

We're free to go. I can't explain how I feel, other than shell-shocked. It's like dreaming wide-awake. Did any of this just happen?

We stand outside the police station. Myself and Dave are going back to our home. Our real home.

Lynne turns to me. 'What do we do now?'

I begin to laugh. So hard that rivers of tears run down my face.

'What do we do now?' I stand with my hand on my hip. 'Are you for fucking real? What you do now is fuck right off. Go and live the life you want, Lynne, because you're totally free.'

'I'll never be free. A person like me is never free.'

'Oh, stop playing the victim, it's getting old,' I snap. 'You're transgender. Get in groups, deal with it. There are plenty of people with problems to face. I'm the mother of a dead baby. We all have masks to put on, faces to portray to the outside world. You've made yourself Lynne. Is she a pathetic victim who blames everyone else for things that result from her own actions? Because that's how it seems. Exactly the same as Jarrod, and Inez before her. Anyway, I couldn't give a fuck what you are. I didn't want you dead, but I know I don't want to see you ever again. So don't stay in that rented house. Move away from me, or I'll make sure you don't get any quality of life here.'

She looks shocked. 'I thought when you asked me to come to your house-,'

'What? That we were becoming friends? You're as fucking mental as Edward. The only reason I asked you to come to my house is so your death wouldn't be on my conscience if he decided you were next.'

'So you do care, or you'd have left me to it.'

I sigh. 'Somewhere in there, is my best friend Jarrod, who I loved dearly. Maybe I tried to save him.

That caring soul who'd do anything for me. Keep that part alive, Lynne.'

I take Dave's arm and walk away.

Leaving her alone for the first time in years.

We stay in our house. It was our family home, and now there's no reason for us to go anywhere else. Edward's body was recovered from the shaft. The earth did him a favour. The police found Jack dead at Bailey's, the same day as the mine accident. It had looked like a suicide. However, Jack had been found in an identical position to Jacobs, raising my suspicions, which I passed on to the detectives. It would appear Jacobs never took his own life after all. Police forensics confirmed that Ed had been responsible for the deaths of both his colleagues.

We've holidayed in Suffolk and Dave and Bobby finally met. They got on well. Bobby showed off his manwhore self, and Dave saw that we were more like brother and sister. That is, how you would imagine a proper brother and sister to be – nothing like my real sibling.

We received a postcard from Lynne. She said she'd moved to a supportive community. That she wouldn't send any more messages but she hoped I'd want to know she was okay and caring for others in a new job as a care worker, and that it was more fulfilling than working at a makeup counter. I threw the card in the recycling bin.

I'm baking biscuits with Millie when there's a knock at the front door. I turn off the hob, and swinging Millie up and into my arms, go to answer it – my paranoia has me looking through the window first.

'Hey there.' A young couple stand on my doorstep. The woman has a bottle of wine in her hand. 'We just moved in down the street, and we're bringing all the neighbours a bottle. Only,' she smiles, 'neighbours don't tend to socialise anymore, and we think that's a shame. We want to bring a sense of community back.'

I look at them. It could have been myself and Jarrod all those years ago.

'I'm sorry, that's kind of you, but I'm really busy.'

'It's only a bottle of wine,' says the woman. She looks at my apron. 'Hey, do you bake? Only I've always wanted to learn to cook.'

'I can't stand wine,' I say, and I shut the door in their faces.

'Grandma, are we going to finish our biscuits off now?' says Millie, her eyes burning with hope.

'We are, darling, and then would you like to make something else because for you I have all the time in the world.'

'When my little sister comes will we still bake?'

Joanne is expecting her second child, another daughter, any day now.

'Yes. We'll still bake. You are my best assistant.'

'Will you let Sarah bake?'

Sarah. That's what Joanne is calling her daughter after taking me to one side to speak with me. A tribute to the daughter who didn't get to live.

'I will, but I'm sure she'll never be as good at it as you are. Now, come on, before the biscuits burn.'

I put her down, and she runs into the kitchen, coming to an abrupt stop in front of the oven. 'I love you, Grandma,' she tells me.

'Love you more, Millie.'

'I don't want to share you, Grandma,' Millie says. 'You're mine.'

## THE END

For suspense updates, sign up to my newsletter:
https://geni.us/andreamlongsuspense

Read on for the descriptions of my other suspenses...

# BULLIED
## ANDREA M. LONG

**Hell hath no fury like a MOTHER scorned.**

CARLA

Marcus Bull. Unremarkable. Unhinged. Un...stoppable?

He made my daughter's life, *my* life, a living hell and got away with it. Broke the rules and stayed smug, hiding behind his tiny tribe, like he was untouchable. I hate him with a passion. It's the only emotion I have left. Hatred.

. . .

And while the police said they could do nothing, I realised that I could do something. Because they taught me, indirectly, how to exact my vengeance.

They say hell hath no fury like a woman scorned. Make that woman a mother and hell shall look like a pilot light, against a mother's inferno. And a mother who no longer has her child? A woman with nothing to lose?

Satan would bow to her.

Get your copy here: https://geni.us/BulLIED

UNDERNEATH
ANDREA M. LONG

**The book that will make you look closely at those around you - including yourself.**

An ordinary life. An extra-ordinary vendetta.

From the outside Lauren's life looks idyllic, yet beneath the surface there are cracks in her marriage.

When an old schoolfriend returns home, Lauren doesn't know whether to avoid her or befriend her. Her husband thinks she should give Bettina a chance; her best friend thinks she has a hidden agenda. A sexy schoolteacher proves an unlikely ally, even if he is an extra threat to her marriage.

Slowly Lauren's life begins to unravel: a car crash and poison-pen letters are just the beginning.

Someone is out to ruin her. But who?

Get your copy here: https://geni.us/Underneath

## SAVE HER
### ANDREA M. LONG

When Eden Stark begins a new job opportunity as a live-in personal assistant, she knows the arrangement with the couple extends beyond simple housework; something she willingly accepts.

But as time goes on, her new employers' possessiveness makes Eden reconsider her position.

Then she goes missing.

Xavier Harrington was the last person to see Eden alive, after a one-night-stand that should have been simple and uncomplicated.

Now the detectives are knocking at his door. But Xavier has his own dark and troubled history.

*Author note: This book contains dark themes, explicit content, and the usual twists you can expect with an Andie M. Long suspense.*

Get your copy here: https://geni.us/SaveHer

# BETRAYAL BEND
ANDREA M. LONG

**Sometimes a good life is not enough…**

Shay Adler and her husband, Cam, run the Brew Love Coffee Company on Liar's Island. A gorgeous couple with sunshine smiles and a perfect marriage.

But behind Shay's smile lies unrest. She loves the husband she met in high school, but sometimes she feels trapped. Trapped by the island, trapped by her marriage and providing stability to her younger sister, and trapped by the whole 'good' ethos that underpins their company.

The tourists provide a distraction. They come, stay a short while, and leave again, and that leaves Shay with opportunities. Ones where she can not be such a good girl.

But on Liar's Island you can trust no one... so Shay's betrayal might not stay secret for long.

*Welcome to Liar's Island... a stand-alone series of interconnected domestic thrillers set in the picture-perfect community of Liars Island. Here, nothing is quite as it seems.*

*On this island, families and friendships are more than meets the eye ... secrets, deceptions, and jealousies threaten to ruin everything these influential people have built. But it isn't only the rich that live here ... and power comes in all shapes and sizes.*

*Everyone here is a liar ... just how far would you go to get what you want?*

Get your copy here: https://geni.us/BetrayalBend

## ABOUT THE AUTHOR

Andrea M. Long writes dark suspense. One minute she's happily walking the dog and the next she's thinking up ways to torture people.

She loves her job.

Andrea lives in Sheffield with her long-suffering partner and son; and Bella, her beautiful Whippet furbaby.

Andrea also writes paranormal romance as Andie M. Long, and contemporary romance as Angel Devlin.

For regular updates join her reader group: https://www.facebook.com/groups/haloandhornshangout

Printed in Great Britain
by Amazon